LP DEA
Dean, John.
No age to die.

DATE DUE

NO AGE TO DIE

John Dean

CHIVERS
THORNDIKE

This Large Print book is published by BBC Audiobooks Ltd, Bath, England and by Thorndike Press®, Waterville, Maine, USA.

Published in 2006 in the U.K. by arrangement with Robert Hale Limited.

Published in 2006 in the U.S. by arrangement with Robert Hale Limited.

U.K. Hardcover ISBN 1–4056–3707–2 (Chivers Large Print)
ISBN 13: 978 1 405 63707 7
U.K. Softcover ISBN 1–4056–3708–0 (Camden Large Print)
ISBN 13: 978 1 405 63708 4
U.S. Softcover ISBN 0–7862–8731–4 (British Favorites)

The text of this Large Print edition is unabridged.
Other aspects of the book may vary from the original edition.

Set in 16 pt. New Times Roman.

Printed in Great Britain on acid-free paper.

British Library Cataloguing in Publication Data available

Library of Congress Cataloging-in-Publication Data

Dean, John, 1961–
    No age to die / by John Dean.
        p.   cm.
    "Thorndike Press large print British favorites."
    ISBN 0–7862–8731–4 (pbk. : alk. paper)
    1. Police—England—Fiction. 2. England—Fiction.
    3. Children—Crimes against—Fiction. 4. Large type books.
    I. Title.
    PR6104.E236N6 2006
    823'.92—dc22   2006009563

When ye have transgressed the covenant of the Lord your God, which he commanded you, and have gone and served other gods, and bowed yourselves to them; then shall the anger of the Lord be kindled against you, and ye shall perish quickly from off the good land which he hath given unto you.

Joshua 23:16

CHAPTER ONE

'It's no age to die,' said Detective Sergeant David Colley, shaking his head and gazing out of the car's rain-flecked windows at the nearby prison.

'Indeed,' grunted Detective Chief Inspector John Blizzard, who was sitting in the driver's seat and staring moodily at the steering-wheel. 'You shouldn't die at fourteen.'

No answer.

'You're supposed to die when your hair has gone white and your joints are creaking.'

Still no reply. It had been like this all morning. The leaden atmosphere outside was nothing compared to the oppressive silence in the car, which had been parked in a terraced street not far from the city centre for two-and-a-half-hours.

'Like you,' added Colley, chancing a mischievous comment in an attempt to lighten the mood and shooting a sly glance at his colleague, eying the flecks of grey in the senior officer's hair.

'Thank you,' muttered Blizzard, the faintest ghost of a smile playing on his lips.

Colley chuckled as he noticed his colleague surreptitiously glance in the rear view mirror and instinctively run a hand across his temples. Probably not even aware he had done it,

1

thought the sergeant. Blizzard's dark mood was entirely understandable. It was a typically gloomy winter's morning in the northern city of Hafton and you never really got used to Hafton's gloomy winter mornings; there was something about the way the damp wheedled its way into your bones. The two men were sitting in Blizzard's ageing Ford Granada—the brass kept trying to get him to change it, went on about corporate image but the chief inspector loved his car and hated corporate images, so that was that.

During their vigil, Blizzard had hardly said a word even though Colley had made occasional attempts to start some kind of conversation to while away the time. Neither of them wanted to be there, but orders were orders and they might as well make the best of it, reasoned the sergeant. But Blizzard was not making the best of it; it was not his style if he didn't like something and he had made clear right at the outset that he had no desire to carry out the task, arguing that there were better ways of occupying police resources. However, the suggestion from his boss, Detective Chief Superintendent Arthur Ronald, that there was plenty of paperwork stacked up on his desk which needed doing, had driven him out into the damp morning air, grumbling for a few minutes before lapsing into the kind of morose silence which Colley knew only too well.

The object of their interest was the large

Victorian prison which stood at the end of the street. A couple of neighbouring cities had recently been given new, gleaming, out-of-town prisons, all fancy designs, glass domes and landscaped grounds, but Hafton still had its Victorian gaol. Victorian in name and culture. Built as a workhouse, it had been used for prisoners for more than a hundred years and, Colley always felt whenever he went in, had probably not been decorated since then. An ageing, crumbling building, with cramped cells and grubby windows and pervaded by the sickly odour of sweat, stale urine and antiseptic, its atmosphere always struck him as dark and oppressive. But it was not so much the smells and the sights which disturbed him, it was the sounds, the rattling of keys, the clanging of the endless doors and the barking of the dogs. The prison was scattered with posters warning that anyone straying within eight feet of a guard's dog would be bitten. Certainly, Colley always sensed a gleam of anticipation in the dogs' eyes and he quickened his pace when walking past the German Shepherds and was always relieved to get out of there.

It was a place ideally suited, Colley thought now as he stared at the gates, to the kind of men who spent so much of their lives there. In a strange way, he felt a kind of sympathy for some of those destined to spend their days inside those walls. He knew they had committed crimes, but to be consigned to that place was, for the sergeant at least, an awful thought. Blizzard, he knew, felt differently. Prison, according to the chief inspector, was the best—the only—place for such people and it was a waste of time if police officers felt any different.

Hafton was a Category A prison, which meant that the men crammed into its dingy cells were lifers, or offenders serving long sentences. You name them, they were there: murderers, armed robbers, drugs traffickers, the lot. In fact, Blizzard and Colley had put a fair few of them away over the years. But Hafton Prison was also notorious because it housed some of the country's most reviled inmates, men hated and despised even by the hardened villains. C wing was where the at-risk prisoners were kept, eighteen of them convicted of serious crimes against children, including murders. And here, any vaguely compassionate feelings were banished in an instant for David Colley. He did not have children—Jay was keen, but Colley didn't fancy the combination of a policeman's hours, an exhausted girlfriend and a screaming baby—however he nevertheless still felt the anger experienced by others when it came to child offenders.

Officers normally cool and calm in the face of death and mayhem found it difficult to control their emotions when confronted by sex offenders, particularly those coppers with children at home. Blizzard shared his colleagues' sentiments: although he had long since been divorced and did not have children, he also felt a deep anger when dealing with such men. Men like Albert Macklin, whose release had brought the detectives to the front gates of Hafton Prison that Friday morning. They didn't come much worse than Albert Macklin. Now aged 67, he had spent thirty-four years in prison on and off, all of it for offences against children, starting with flashing at small boys in the park and building up, with a sense of inevitability which the criminal justice system seemed incapable of preventing, to the murder of a teenager.

'How come he's being let out anyway?' asked Colley, musing out loud and sensing a slight change in Blizzard's demeanour, a lightening that meant he might be amenable to conversation.

'A good question,' said the chief inspector, turning to look at him with a fierceness in his eyes. 'If it was down to me, they would have thrown away the key a long time ago.'

Colley surveyed him for a moment or two. The sergeant knew why Blizzard felt like that: the officer had particular reason to remember Albert Macklin, who had been gaoled eighteen years previously for a murder that had shocked a city that thought it had become inured to the outrages of those who lurked in its shadows.

As a young uniformed officer having only been in the force a relatively short time, Blizzard had been one of the team which took part in the search of the frozen canalside for clues after the ubiquitous person walking their dog—why was it always people walking their dogs? wondered Colley idly—found the body of 14-year-old Danny Maddox, concealed beneath a hide of hurriedly constructed branches.

It did not take the murder team long to come a-knocking on Albert Macklin's door. Even though he had managed to keep out of trouble for a couple of years following his release from prison, a man with a record like his was always the first to come under suspicion. At first Macklin denied enticing the teenager to the canal-side, claiming Danny Maddox had been a willing participant in a sex game. The boy, claimed Macklin, had become frightened and tried to run away. According to Macklin, he panicked, frightened that the teenager would tell the police and condemn him to another stretch in prison, so he grabbed a branch which was lying nearby and struck the boy. Danny Maddox had fallen and hit his head. All a horrible accident.

Except the post-mortem revealed that Danny Maddox had been struck seven times, not once as Macklin claimed, and detectives proved that the stick was unlikely to have come from that area because those particular trees did not grow there. Macklin retracted his story in interview and admitted the lot. The judge sentenced him to life with a recommendation to serve at least twenty years. Although the judge had talked grandly about protecting the community, good behaviour meant Macklin was now due out, and the reason the detectives were waiting outside the prison. Shortly after ten o'clock the gates swung open slowly and a small man emerged tentatively, looking about him as if unsure what to do next.

'That's him,' said Blizzard, a touch of urgency in his voice.

They surveyed the man for a moment. Dressed in a dishevelled baggy brown suit which might have been fashionable once, he seemed somehow crumpled, his legs bandy, his back slightly stooped, his white hair wispy and receding, his cheeks hollow and sunken, with a faded two inch scar on the right one and his bony chin speckled with stubble. He looked like any other little old man, but any thought that he was harmless was dispelled by the mouth, thin, cruel and revealing crooked yellowing teeth when the lips parted, and the clear blue glinting eyes, which darted from side to side, reminding Colley of a snake seeking its prey. This man, thought the sergeant feeling a shiver run down his spine, was dangerous.

'Jesus,' he breathed.

'Indeed,' said Blizzard. 'Now you try to tell

7

me that this man should be allowed out. Come on, let's get it over with.'

They got out of the car and walked down the street towards Albert Macklin, who was still standing, continuing to look somewhat bewildered, in front of the prison. His expression as he watched them approach was hostile and suspicious.

'Macklin,' said Blizzard, his voice suddenly harsh, 'I am Detective Chief Inspector John Blizzard, of Hafton Police.'

'What happened to Dennis Barry?' asked Macklin, in his strangely high-pitched voice, referring to the detective who had arrested him.

'You've been away a long time,' retorted Blizzard, irritated by the use of the first name. *Detective Chief Inspector* Barry retired eight years ago. He died last year.'

'Couldn't have happened to a nicer man,' said Macklin, a thin smile playing on his lips. 'So what do you want with me?'

'It's a friendly warning,' said Blizzard, fixing him with a steely glare. 'This is my patch now and I will be watching you like a hawk. One wrong move and you'll be back inside that fast your feet won't touch. If I were you, I'd leave the city.'

'What! Just because you say so?'

There was outrage in the voice but no sincerity: Macklin was playing the game.

'There's a lot of people would like to have a

8

go at you,' said Blizzard, adding with a menacing smile, 'And we might not be able to stop them, eh, Sergeant?'

'Can't be watching your back all the time,' nodded Colley.

'But I've served my time, why would anyone—?' began Macklin innocently.

'Don't play the fool with me,' snapped Blizzard. 'You know damn well that once word spreads that you are out, Danny Maddox's family will come looking for you. Bob Maddox has already tried to have you killed once, so I suggest—'

'You are in no position to suggest anything,' interrupted a young man, stepping quickly in front of the startled detectives. 'Albie is coming with me and where he goes is none of your business.'

'I doubt even his mother called him Albie,' retorted Blizzard, surveying the bespectacled man in his early twenties, who had lank brown hair, a freckled face, brown cords and a leather jacket with patches on the elbows. 'Do you mind telling me who the bloody hell you are?'

'My name is David Reed. I work for Take-Out.'

'I'll have a cheese sandwich then,' said Blizzard sardonically. 'What about you, Sergeant?'

'Actually, it's linked to St Mary's Church,' explained Colley, not attempting to stifle the grin. 'It's a hostel for ex-offenders.'

9

'Oh, yes, I heard about it,' sighed Blizzard. 'That's all the old rogue needs. Some bloody yoghurt-knitting Bible-bashers looking after him.'

'I'll thank you to keep your prejudices to yourself,' said David Reed archly. 'Albie will be staying with us until he can find his feet.'

'Hopefully he will find them walking out of the city,' grunted Blizzard.

'He will be staying at our hostel,' said the young man, taking Macklin by the arm and starting to lead him to a battered orange Citroen car before turning and shouting, 'And I'll thank you to stay away from him, Chief Inspector.'

'Little toerag,' muttered Blizzard as he watched them go. 'What is the world coming to, David?'

'Dunno,' replied the sergeant. 'And after you were so friendly with the nice young yoghurt-knitting Bible-basher as well.'

'And how come it is allowed to run a hostel for people like Macklin next to a church where kids go?' asked Blizzard, pointedly ignoring the comment.

'There was a bit of publicity in the paper,' recalled Colley. 'But it died down after a day or two.'

They watched as the Citroen spluttered into life and drove past them, Macklin in the passenger seat, smirking and waving regally as he surveyed the detectives.

'Cheeky git,' humphed Blizzard, then, recovering his composure, said: 'Well, at least we've done our bit. The brass wanted the old beggar warned and we've warned him. Time, I think, David, for some breakfast. I rather fancy a bacon butty from Maeve's café.'

'Actually,' remarked the sergeant slyly, following behind him towards the car, 'Jay's always trying to get me to eat more healthily so thought I might have some yoghurt.'

'You'll like traffic duty,' shouted Blizzard, but Colley could see from the heaving shoulders that he had appreciated the joke.

The sergeant chuckled. Perhaps it wasn't going to be such a bad day after all.

CHAPTER TWO

Colley was wrong. It was a bad day—although it took a few hours for things to unravel. After leaving the prison, the officers found themselves separated, Blizzard heading with many a grumble to attend another of the interminable strategy meetings at force headquarters, Colley to investigate a series of burglaries against businesses on one of the division's industrial estates. By the end of the day, however, Blizzard's prediction about Albert Macklin's safety had come true, and, as so often happened, the phone call came just as he had pulled on his jacket and snapped off the office light before heading for home through the gathering darkness of a typically dank Hafton autumn afternoon. Blizzard stood in the door for a moment, silhouetted in the light from the corridor, and wondered whether or not to answer it. He knew he would, but he always liked to go through the ritual anyway. It was one of those little things that had helped keep him sane during well over twenty years as a police officer.

John Blizzard was 46. Dressed as usual in dark suit with tie dangling loosely, he had tousled brown hair, was clean-shaven with a tendency towards shadow in late afternoon, had a rounded face with slight bags under the clear blue eyes and wrinkles on his forehead, which became more pronounced when he was under pressure—which was most of the time in the western division. He had always worked in Hafton, virtually all of it plain-clothes, and had been promoted to take charge of the division's CID four years previously following a series of extremely difficult inquiries, including one which had resulted in a gang of armed robbers being jailed for seventy nine years between them for attacks carried out in four counties. It had earned him his seventh commendation and his eighth death threat. Blizzard always valued the death threats more, a reliable sign, he reasoned, of a detective doing his job properly. Indeed, some colleagues sensed that

12

he was proud of them. It was the kind of attitude which led some to describe him as arrogant; those who knew him well begged to differ.

Blizzard's office was in Abbey Road Police Station, opened in the 1960s, supposedly as a temporary measure and still there three decades later, green paint peeling, windows grimy and roof leaking. During the previous winter, one of the prefabs had been ripped off its foundations during gales, but even then a replacement was not forthcoming and they simply patched the building up. The accountants had been promising the funds for a new police station for years, but chief constables came and chief constables went and nothing ever happened so the officers and civilians continued to broil in the summer and freeze in the winter because there was only a clapped-out old air conditioning system and a heater which broke down every two weeks. The officers of Abbey Road knew the heating engineers better than they knew some of the senior officers from headquarters.

Not that any of this worried John Blizzard because he spent too much time out and about, meeting the many and varied demands of the division, to care much about the quality of the decor in his office. The western division was an area of sharp contrast. On its western fringes, the city outskirts, were the plush suburbs with their gravel drives, huge houses and outdoor swimming pools, owned by self-made businessmen and women, aviation company executives from the large plant in the city and the odd villain who hid behind the respectable façade provided by a pinstripe suit and briefcase.

Separated from them by a dwindling green strip, steadily disappearing beneath box-like new housing as the council sold off sports fields like there was no tomorrow, was the other side to the division, the run-down '60s council estates with their smashed windows, overgrown front gardens and burnt-out cars. Next to them, creating a buffer zone between the residential areas and the bright lights of the city centre, were the older streets with their rows of shabby Victorian terraces, most of them owned by landlords and populated by DSS 'clients', as the bureaucrats liked to call them. Blizzard had another word but tended not to utter it when in the company of the top brass.

Overshadowing them were 1970s tower blocks designed by town planners who had talked excitedly about cities in the sky at the time but did not bother to check what it was like up there. Pretty plans did not translate into pretty reality and, as time passed, their concrete crumbled and with it the architects' dream as the blocks were taken over by drug addicts and petty criminals. The city council talked endlessly about regeneration partnerships and funding initiatives and appointed chinless wonders to champion the dream, but nothing seemed to change and the drug dealers and the pimps continued to ply their trade and taunt the police whenever they came to make an arrest.

The local paper called the estates no-go areas but Blizzard and Ronald, his direct superior and long-time friend, who had overall responsibility for the CID in the south of the county, sent detectives in whenever they could. They were making a point, they said, whenever challenged by senior officers worried about the risk of civil disturbance. The western division had a large, and growing, drugs problem, heroin mainly, but recently showing signs of Yardie infiltration with a number of crack houses, had an ingrained prostitution problem and a murder rate that was higher than it should be and, against that backdrop, they argued that firm police action was needed, whoever it disturbed.

So when Blizzard picked up the telephone in his office that evening, he knew it was unlikely to be good news. It was David Colley, another bad sign.

'You may want to get out to Lewis Street,' said the sergeant.

'Why, what's happened?'

'It seems the locals have worked out that Albert Macklin is out.'

'Marvellous,' sighed Blizzard. 'I'll meet you

in the car-park.'

Twenty minutes later, having weaved their way through the Friday night rush-hour traffic, Blizzard and Colley were in Lewis Street, part of the network of shabby side streets not far from the city centre. They were standing outside St Mary's Church, a modern church sporting a large stained-glass window adorned with a modern representation of Jesus on the Cross, and for some reason, an armoured tank standing in front of him, atop of which was a soldier pointing a gun at the Lord. Next to the tank was a depiction of Mother Teresa. The window had been unveiled a year or so before but none of it had impressed Blizzard. He had thrown down the newspaper and grunted that, as far as he could recall, Mother Teresa had never visited the western division, and that if she had, the likelihood was that someone would have nicked her handbag.

But the detectives were not looking at the window this time, rather at the large group of men, women and children outside the church, shouting angrily and wielding hurriedly made posters bearing slogans like. We don't want no perverts'.

'Don't you hate ungrammatical protests?' murmured Blizzard.

Colley did not reply. None was needed. There had always been an easy working relationship between the two men. At 36, Colley had found himself increasingly assisting

16

Blizzard with major inquiries over the past three years, usually at the DCI's request. Today, as always, Colley's black hair was neatly combed, his round, almost boyish, face showed no signs of stubble, and his black trousers, blue shirt and grey jacket had all been perfectly ironed by Jay. His shoes shone as usual.

Blizzard gestured at a single-storey, flat-roofed red-brick building next to the church.

'Do I assume that is where the yoghurt people live?' he asked sardonically, noticing without surprise that a couple of the windows had been smashed.

'That's the Take-Out hostel,' nodded Colley.

Glancing at the two nervous young uniformed officers standing in front of the building and eying the ugly crowd with growing unease, Blizzard asked, 'So when did all this blow up?'

'Control Room got a call half an hour ago from David Reed, the—'

'The yoghurt-knitter.'

'Yeah. He said someone had chucked a couple of bricks through the window and that a few ne'er-do-wells were hanging around outside. By the time the uniforms got here, this lot had showed up.'

'Exactly who are the uniforms?' asked Blizzard, eying them sourly. 'Look like a couple of rejects from the bloody Boy Scouts.'

'New lads,' said Colley. 'Only been in the job a few weeks.'

It's come to something when coppers look young even to other coppers,' sighed Blizzard. He groaned as he spotted a face in the crowd.

'Marvellous,' he sighed. 'Do you recognize the big fellow in the front row?'

'Nope.'

'That is Bob Maddox . . .'

'The dead kid's dad?'

'If by "the dead kid" you mean Danny Maddox,' said Blizzard archly, 'then you are correct. He stood up in the public gallery when Albert Macklin was sentenced and threatened to kill him. Word was he got a couple of his mates to try when Macklin was inside. He got stabbed with a broken bottle . . .'

'Is that where he got the scar from?'

'Yes; one of the warders found him and saved him from bleeding to death.' Blizzard set off towards the shouting protestors. 'Pity really.'

'How do you know Bob Maddox?' asked Colley, scuttling after him.

'Nicked him a few years ago for stealing cars. Nasty piece of work. Come on, let's sort this out.' He raised a hand and bellowed, 'Shut up, the lot of you!'

The crowd went silent.

'Thank you,' he said, surveying the angry faces then fixing his expression on Bob

Maddox, a large man of eighteen stone, in his early fifties, with a skinhead cut, squat features, a bull neck and dressed in an ill-fitting white T-shirt and filthy jeans. 'Now, since I assume this is not a Bible class, I think I can guess what this is about. Want to tell me what you hope to achieve, Bob?'

'It ain't right, Mr Blizzard,' scowled Maddox, to murmurs of agreement from the crowd. 'He took my son's life.'

'And paid the price,' said Blizzard evenly.

'You don't really believe that,' said Maddox, jabbing an accusing finger at the detective. 'You think he's scum just like we do.'

'My personal views do not come into it: you lot smashing windows does. For your information, we talked with Albert Macklin this morning and suggested it was unwise to return to the city.'

'Too bloody right it is,' shouted a man from the back of the crowd.

'But the fact remains that Albert Macklin is a free man,' added Blizzard calmly. 'And the people that run this hostel have offered him a temporary home—whatever we may think of the wisdom of such a move.'

It was then that the flash illuminated the scene, startling everyone. Stepping forward out of the gathering evening gloom, a photographer from the local evening newspaper had started taking pictures of the confrontation. Standing next to him was a reporter, a scruffy young man in a green anorak.

'Who invited you?' snapped Blizzard.

'I did,' said a voice coolly, and a woman stepped forward and extended an elegant hand. 'My name is Margaret Hatton.'

Blizzard ignored the hand and eyed her dubiously. Margaret Hatton was not like the other people in the crowd. A tall, dark-haired woman in her late forties, her face was angular and intelligent, the blue eyes sharp and keen. Smartly dressed in a dark business suit, her demeanour suggested someone who was completely in control of herself and determined to get her own way. Not classically attractive, thought Blizzard, but there was nevertheless something about her. In another situation, he might even have fancied her himself. Colley watched the confrontation with interest: Blizzard had never been particularly good at dealing with pushy women—and this woman looked pushy as hell.

'And who might you be?' asked Blizzard archly, banishing thoughts of her attractiveness.

'I am the chair of P3. I came up from our Buckinghamshire headquarters this afternoon.'

'And in English, P3 would be what, exactly?' asked Blizzard, suspicious as ever of trendy names.

'Protect, Prevent and Punish. We were created to ensure that decent people are protected from paedophiles like Albert Macklin wherever they are in the country.'

'Decent people like them?' asked Blizzard, raising an eyebrow as he glanced at the gathering behind him, in particular Bob Maddox's bovine features and the flattened nose of his eldest son, a burly thug in his late twenties whom his officers had locked up twice for unprovoked attacks in city pubs.

An ugly murmur ran round the crowd.

'They have rights, too,' said Margaret Hatton, refusing to rise to the bait.

'So, what do you hope to achieve by being here?' asked Blizzard curtly, nodding to the pressmen. 'And by bringing them along? It can only inflame an already difficult situation.'

'We want Albert Macklin to leave this city,' said Margaret Hatton firmly.

'Don't we all,' sighed Blizzard, trying to ignore his developing headache.

'And we don't like the fact that the Church is helping him,' she added, 'and that children go to this church. We think that paedophiles should not be allowed somewhere like this.'

'Well, at least we can agree on something.'

Just then David Reed, his hair even oilier than when they had seen him before, his face ashen and his eyes wide behind his spectacles, emerged from the Take-Out hostel and ventured over to the crowd.

'I demand protection,' he said to Blizzard, in a tremulous voice. 'This mob tried to kill

Albie.'

More angry murmurs from the crowd.

'So you want our help now, do you?' asked Blizzard pointedly. 'However, I don't think a couple of bricks represents trying to kill the old goat.'

'You must do something,' urged the young man earnestly. 'Someone could be—'

'I have warned them to keep away from this place,' interrupted Blizzard in a voice which suggested the conversation was at an end. 'And might I suggest that you, for your part, do your bit to keep the peace by making sure that come tomorrow morning Albert Macklin is on his way out of Hafton.'

'That's not fair,' exclaimed Reed. 'How can we help him rehabilitate if—?'

But his protestations were drowned out by more angry shouts from the crowd and they surged forward. It was only the nimble actions of David Colley—the two wide-eyed rookie uniformed officers appearing to be rooted to the spot—that saved the church worker from serious harm as he plucked him out of the way of the mob. Seconds later, the protestors were heading towards the front door of the building, intent on finding Albert Macklin.

'Take one more step!' hollered Blizzard, recovering from his surprise, 'and I will arrest the lot of you!'

His words had an instantaneous effect. The crowd turned to eye him uncertainly, wondering if he was bluffing. One look at his steely glare was enough and one by one, they slunk back onto the street, Bob Maddox and his son the last ones to go. Colley walked quietly over to the son and nimbly snatched the half brick from his grasp before he had even realized what was happening. Maddox Junior looked as if he was about to protest, but Colley held up a finger to his lips and the young man thought better of it.

'Go home,' said Blizzard. 'This building will have a police guard all night and I hope that when everyone is calmer we can work this out. Now go.'

After a nod from Margaret Hatton, the crowd started to slip away all except Bob Maddox and his son who hesitated a moment longer.

'Bob,' said Blizzard, with a tone of warning in his voice.

Maddox seemed to crumple.

'He killed my boy, Mr Blizzard,' he said in a low voice, and the detectives were surprised to see tears starting in the eyes of this bull-necked monster of a man. 'He was fourteen. It's no age to die.'

'No, it isn't,' said Blizzard, his tone suddenly softer, and placing a hand on his arm. 'But getting yourself locked up for someone like that won't do anyone any good, will it now?'

Maddox shook his head and after a moment or two turned and ambled off into the night, followed closely by his meat-head son. Blizzard turned to Margaret Hatton.

'There is a danger that your presence will fuel disorder here,' he said.

'I will not cease my campaign,' she said firmly, and her voice also changed from the harsh one of confrontation to a gentler, sadder tone. 'I am like Mr Maddox, Chief Inspector. A man like Albert Macklin also killed *my* son. I cannot sleep knowing that these types of people are being let out of prison and I will not cease campaigning for their return.'

'Do you want to say anything to the press, Chief Inspector?' asked the reporter, stepping forward, notebook at the ready.

'Not really,' replied Blizzard curtly.

'But—'

'But nothing. Now sod off before I have one of the Boy Scouts check your tyres.'

The reporter opened his mouth to object, thought better of it and he and the cameraman walked off, shooting occasional angry glances over their shoulders at the chief inspector.

'I've got a bad feeling about this, David,' said Blizzard grimly, watching Margaret Hatton catch up the pressmen and start talking earnestly to them. 'A really bad feeling. This is only the start.'

He turned to David Reed. 'I told you this morning that I want Macklin out of this city by tomorrow,' he said curtly, and caught a glimpse of the killer's face peering out of a window in the hostel, 'because next time, I am not sure that we can stop them tearing him limb from limb.'

'It goes against everything we believe,' objected the church worker. 'When he was on the Cross, our Lord—'

'Sod your Lord!' snapped Blizzard. 'You may think you are doing something important here, but I am telling you that if Macklin stays, someone will get to him . . . and probably won't care if they knock your head off to do it.'

With that he spun on his heel and stalked across the street to his car. David Reed looked hopefully at Colley.

'Can't you talk some sense into him?' he asked.

'He's right on this one,' said the sergeant. 'Albert Macklin is trouble. He has no place in this city.'

And he followed Blizzard across the street, leaving a disconsolate David Reed standing in front of the broken windows, watched impassively by the two rookie uniforms preparing for a long, cold night on sentry duty. As the detective's Ford Granada car edged out of the street, the rain began to fall again.

CHAPTER THREE

'Like you said,' murmured Blizzard, his voice a hardly audible croak, 'no age to die.' There was no reply from David Colley. None was needed. Words would not have been enough anyway. It was dusk on a drizzly Sunday, two days after the confrontation outside the church, and the detectives were standing on the towpath running alongside Hafton Canal, looking down at the body of a teenage boy, head stoved in, face partly concealed by dried blood, limbs splayed awkwardly, forearms scratched, blue T-shirt ripped, jeans covered in mud, all the signs of a desperate battle for life against his attacker. He had been found by an angler—the man walking his dog must have been on a day-off, Colley had thought sardonically, before reminding himself sharply of the gravity of the situation in which they found themselves.

The fisherman, having spent all Sunday fishing on the canal bank, had been wending his way home for tea shortly after five o'clock when he noticed a foot sticking out from beneath the undergrowth. Hardly daring to breathe, he had investigated further and found, to his horror, the body of a young boy, partly concealed by branches hurriedly snapped off nearby bushes and trees.

Not particularly well concealed though, approaching winter having claimed most of the leaves by now. Having sat for ten minutes, shocked, numbed, unable to move, the angler had roused himself enough to use his mobile phone to ring the police.

Within twenty minutes, the canal bank was swarming with officers, John Blizzard and David Colley among them. As they stood surveying the body, which was being examined by forensics officers and Home Office pathologist Peter Reynolds, Detective Sergeant Dave Tulley was taking a statement from the fisherman, a man in his fifties, who sat on a nearby log, shaking badly and trying to form words to describe what he had seen. Colley also shivered, not from shock but from the biting wind which was sweeping along the canal. He turned up his anorak collar and looked around him, peering into an inky blackness pierced only by the flashing blue lights on the police cars and the pale glow from factories on the industrial estate on the far side of the canal.

Hafton Canal had once been the lifeblood of the city, used to ferry the textiles and wool products to the major conurbations further inland in the early 1800s. The advent of railways had, however, diminished its importance and by the middle of the twentieth century it was hardly used by anyone, falling into neglect, its locks unused, the operating

27

gear seized up and rusted, its water levels gradually dropping as weeds slowly choked out its life. A symbol, many said, of the terminal decline of the city. Ten years ago, however, it had been purchased by a group of keen volunteers who had raised the money to bring it back into life, clearing away the vegetation, restoring the water flows, stocking it with fish and encouraging leisure boat use. A symbol, some said, of the regeneration of the city.

All the headlines had been good ones, until now, thought Colley glancing over to the local newspaper crime reporter and photographer standing beyond the tape stretched across the canal bank by the police. It was the same team which had covered the protest outside the hostel and splashed it all over the front page the next day.

'How did they get here so quickly?' asked Colley curiously.

'Not sure,' said Blizzard grimly, 'and at the moment, I do not care. Do we know who this kid is?'

'We think it's a lad called Josh Holdsworth,' replied Colley, returning his attention to the body. 'Mum rang in earlier in the day saying he had not returned home for Sunday lunch. She's on her way down.'

'How old?'

'Fourteen. Left home this morning to play football with his mates but, according to mum, their game finished at twelve. His mates

28

thought he was going home.'

'Would he have walked home via the canal?'

'Possibly. He lived near the church. Didn't Danny M—'

'Yes,' nodded Blizzard, 'Danny Maddox lived near the church.'

'And isn't—?'

'Yes,' and Blizzard turned away and stared soberly into the night. 'This is where Danny Maddox was found. And before you ask, yes, Albert Macklin did cover his victim with branches.'

'Jesus,' murmured Colley. 'You don't think Albert Macklin did this, do you?'

'Who knows?' shrugged Blizzard, his gaze fixed on some distant point in the dark waters of the canal.

'According to that do-gooder at Take-Out, Macklin left the city yesterday morning after our little chat,' said Colley. 'Went to stay with relatives in Derby. Told his parole officer the same thing.'

'But did he?' asked Blizzard sharply, turning round to face his sergeant.

'Who knows?' shrugged Colley. 'David Reed didn't know their names and Derby police are asking around but haven't come up with anything.'

'Then I suggest you ring them again,' said Blizzard, jerked from his reveries and suddenly energized, 'because I want Albert Macklin back in this city pdq!'

29

'I'm sure he will appreciate the irony,' remarked Colley.

'I don't care what he appreciates! Find the bastard before someone else gets killed!'

And with that John Blizzard strode off down the tow path.

CHAPTER FOUR

Ten o'clock that night found John Blizzard back at Abbey Road Police Station, sipping tea from a steaming mug while tipping back on his seat in Arthur Ronald's office. A grimacing Ronald was on the phone, being talked at by the chief constable, who had made the call after getting in from a charity night at the golf club. Blizzard chuckled as he saw the detective chief superintendent's discomfort. Ronald flapped a hand frantically and glared at him. Blizzard watched his superior officer with affection. There were few people in the job that John Blizzard could say he truly liked: David Colley was one, Arthur Ronald was another.

He and Blizzard went back a long way, having first worked together as rookie uniform officers, then in CID, before their careers went different ways. Blizzard remained a detective, spurning the chance of further promotion if he went into uniform; Ronald readily donned the blue and rose rapidly through the ranks. They had eventually been reunited at Abbey Road as Ronald, gratefully, returned to his CID roots and assumed overall command of the southern half of the county.

They were very different characters. Indeed, it was probably that difference that made their friendship work. University-educated Ronald, married, with two children, was a slightly pudgy, balding man with ruddy cheeks and eyes with bags sagging underneath them. A man given to constant worrying about mortgages and school fees, he looked older than his forty-eight years. A smart dresser with a sharply pressed suit, tie always done up and shoes shined, he was a charming man with an easy manner and a gift for the kind of diplomacy he was currently exhibiting with the chief constable, who was demanding to know what he was doing about the murder.

Blizzard had different qualities: having gone straight into the police from school, he had a diffident way with people and a habit of saying what he thought, usually to the wrong person at the wrong time. It was probably what did for his marriage, he always said. Whatever the reason, his wife had walked out and he had not heard from her in the seven years since. Heard plenty from her lawyer, mind. That evening, Blizzard had on his usual clothes, a slightly crumpled black suit, the trousers flecked with mud from the canal bank, a red tie hanging loosely around his neck, and perennially scuffed shoes. Ronald, eying him while letting the chief constable rant, was filled with a desire, as was so often the case, to toss a comb at Blizzard and order him to run it through his tousled brown hair. But he didn't. He knew he never would. Blizzard would have only tossed it back at him with a sardonic gleam in his eye.

Neither man had been idle in the five hours since the discovery of Josh Holdsworth's body. Blizzard had immediately assumed control of the inquiry, overseeing what little could be done on the canal bank in the darkness—a full search would resume when daylight broke in the morning—and identifying lines of inquiry. He had sent Colley and a woman police officer to talk to the boy's distraught mother: the teenager's father worked on the oil rigs and was travelling back that night. None of the inquiries, though, had yielded much information.

Later in the evening, Blizzard had briefed Ronald and the senior man had arranged a press conference for the following morning, something neither was particularly looking forward to but which both acknowledged was a necessary evil if they were to appeal for public help. This was one of those cases where it looked like it would be needed because, apart from the angler, they had struggled to find anyone who was on the canal during the later afternoon. And both were acutely aware that if you didn't solve a murder within the first few hours, it usually became a protracted affair.

'So what did the chief have to say?' asked Blizzard, lowering the legs of the chair onto the floor and leaning forward to place his drained mug on the desk as Ronald replaced the receiver.

'Panicking as usual,' replied Ronald, reaching for his own tea, taking a swallow and grimacing when he realized it had gone cold.

'Worried what people will think,' commented Blizzard sardonically. 'He won't get his Queen's Police Medal with dead boys turning up on his patch. And you'll be off his Christmas card list.'

Ronald fixed him with what was supposed to be icy stare but all it illicited was another chuckle from Blizzard.

'You know,' sighed Ronald, feigning disappointment, 'sometimes I get the impression that you do not give me the respect my rank demands.'

Blizzard smiled.

'So,' said Ronald, his mood changing, suddenly business-like, 'do we fancy Albert Macklin for this one?'

'It's a hell of coincidence if we don't, same stretch of canal, same MO, same method of covering up the body. Reynolds is going to do a full post-mortem tomorrow, but he confirmed that probable cause of death is a head injury. Reckons Josh Holdsworth was

33

struck with a large piece of wood. Hopefully we will find the weapon tomorrow.'

'And Macklin, where is he?'

'Over the hills and far away. Colley checked the church hostel and he's not there and he put another call into Derby Police a few minutes ago but they haven't got anywhere. One of their detectives has been checking Macklins there but none of them knows our guy. Besides, there is no evidence that he even has family in Derby. Could have made the whole lot up.'

'So there's not much we can do before morning then?'

'Not really. Might as well head for home . . .'

'Afraid not, gentlemen,' said Colley, walking into the room and giving them an apologetic look. 'Seems the locals have taken things into their own hands!'

CHAPTER FIVE

'This is all we need,' said Blizzard grimly, standing in the casualty unit of the general hospital and glancing at Colley.

It was past eleven o'clock and the unit was relatively quiet, as was often the case on a Sunday night, a blessed relief after the usual weekend of mayhem in the city centre. Adding to that weekend's problems had been the fact that many people had received their monthly pay packets on the Thursday which meant young men and women had headed for the nightspots with plenty of money to spend. Hafton was a typical northern city centre, a mixture of traditional pubs used by the flat-cap and whippet brigade, all fug and ferrets, garish bars with happy hours and cheap cocktails, frequented by the bright young things who did not seem to possess coats, and a few nightclubs policed by mean and moody bouncers in black leather jackets and sunglasses, tough men who made up the rules as they went along and did not welcome the intervention of the boys in blue when trouble broke out.

That weekend had been pretty routine for the city centre division, three stabbings, one serious, none fatal, four men taken to hospital with head injuries after a brawl on a street corner, two young women brought in to have their stomachs pumped out after drinking too much and fourteen arrests for various drunken antics. Seven years previously, Blizzard had been approached by one of the brass to ask if he would be prepared to switch to uniform in the city centre in return for a fast-track to promotion. It had been tempting—for about two seconds. Blizzard was highly rated, despite his outspoken tendencies, was ambitious and also had a mortgage to pay on a nice detached house in a village on the western edge of the city. At the time he had been one of the two detective inspectors responsible for a a whole series of sprawling housing estates on the ever-expanding eastern edge of Hafton. The pay was not brilliant, the hours were long, the work was unforgiving and for a few moments he considered the move seriously. Then he thought about the city centre with its posturing young bucks and shrill mini-skirted women, all tanked up to the eyeballs, and he thought of the streams of urine trickling across the pavements and he declined the offer. He knew it was not for him, however short the posting might have been.

It had been a good call. Within a few months, he had been switched to the western division as detective inspector and was promoted to detective chief inspector three years later. All those memories came flooding back now as he and Colley stood in casualty waiting for the staff nurse to finish patching up an elderly cyclist who had gashed his head when he toppled off his bike on the way home from the pub.

'Sorry about that,' she said, waving at the old guy as he tottered towards the front doors. 'You wanted to know about young Mr Reed?'

'Yes,' nodded Blizzard. 'I understand he has serious head injuries?'

How those injuries came to be inflicted was, at the moment, a mystery. The detectives had done a detour on the way to the hospital and visited the hostel at St Mary's Church where a trembling woman who announced herself to be Glenda Rutherford, the assistant night manager, told them that shortly before ten o'clock another rock had been thrown at the hostel, this time shattering the window of the office in which David Reed had been catching up on paperwork. The rock struck him on the back of the head and the terrified woman had rushed in to find him sprawled on the floor with blood pouring from an ugly wound just above the hairline. Her frantic attempts to gain a response from him had failed and she had called an ambulance. The rock was still on the floor of the office when the detectives arrived and was now being examined by forensics.

'He is very poorly,' said the nurse. 'We are waiting to see his X-rays in case he has a fractured skull. It seems likely.'

'Will he live?'

'I don't think his injuries are life-threatening,' said the nurse. 'We'll know better when the doctor has had a look at his X-rays.'

'Can we talk to him?' asked Colley, knowing the answer.

'Maybe in a day or two but definitely not now. I think your Mr Reed has had enough excitement for one night, don't you?' and the nurse smiled sweetly and headed off to deal with a teenager who was being brought in by two uniform officers after being assaulted on his way home. Blood poured from his nose, to which he was clutching a handkerchief already stained crimson.

'Come on,' sighed Blizzard, heading towards the door, 'we can't do anything else here.'

'Got to be Bob Maddox, hasn't it?' said Colley, as they walked down the stairs—Blizzard would have happily used the lift but the sergeant was on a mission to persuade the chief inspector that he needed to take more exercise to help reduce his thickening wasteline.

'Fair bet,' nodded Blizzard. 'He's pretty wound up about things. Let's check him out in the morning, though. The nurse is right, there has been enough excitement for one day.'

As the officers walked across the car park, they noticed without much surprise that it was raining again.

CHAPTER SIX

'Well?' asked Blizzard impatiently.

'He's dead,' replied Reynolds, in that strangely nasal voice of his, straightening up and grinning at the chief inspector's pained expression.

Reynolds was the wrong person to have to deal with on a Monday morning. There were some people in life that you do not like—well, in Blizzard's case there was a whole bunch of them—and Peter Reynolds was pretty near the top of his list. Indeed, the detective even disliked him more than some villains. You knew where you were with a villain, he often told himself after feeling a collar, but you just did not know where you were sometimes with the medical profession. Reynolds was the Home Office pathologist, a man who appeared to have little time for people when they were living but found them suddenly fascinating when they were dead.

The thing Blizzard found most difficult to fathom, as he watched the pathologist eagerly probing the teenager's body on the slab in his sparse examination room, was the gusto with which Reynolds did his job. A balding middle-aged little man with piggy eyes twinkling out of a chubby face, the pathologist absolutely loved post-mortems and, even more than that, he loved post-mortems with police officers present because he knew that they hated the whole experience, hated the blood, hated the cutting of flesh and, above all things, hated the stomach-churning smell. Reynolds had grown used to it years ago. That police officers hadn't was a constant joy to him. Blizzard and Colley were among the better ones and, having arrived a couple of moments ago, they had watched him without showing undue stress while he completed his work on Josh Holdsworth.

'Cut the stage act,' rasped Blizzard, acutely

aware that he was soon due to attend what would be a difficult press conference and that he needed something to tell the journalists. 'What killed him?'

'Well, I've got a surprise for you,' said Reynolds, running a hand absent-mindedly across the teenager's battered skull.

'You don't say you are going to be helpful?' muttered Blizzard, watching the pathologist's wandering hand with distaste.

Colley smiled slightly. He loved the meetings between the two men. He knew that Blizzard detested the examiner, regarding him as insensitive and crass. Reynolds, for his part, knew exactly how Blizzard viewed him and did like to play his little games, something he knew infuriated the detective.

'He was killed with something red.'

'Red,' exclaimed Blizzard. 'The search teams didn't find anything red at the scene this morning. Just branches and a few pieces of concrete. Are you sure it's red?'

'I am,' nodded Reynolds. 'Look.'

He held up some minute shards which glinted under the harsh lights of the post-mortem room.

'Where were they?' asked Colley, peering closer.

'In his skull. They're wood. There is no doubt that they came from the murder weapon. Must have been fairly heavy and wielded with some force. The trauma to the

40

brain is extensive. But probably just one blow.'

'Any other injuries?' asked the sergeant.

'One or two.' Reynolds held up the boy's right forearm to reveal a couple of small scratches. 'I might have expected more, though. Maybe he was caught by surprise . . .'

'Maybe.'

'There are older injuries as well.'

'Like?'

'Scars, as if he has been struck with something sharp—a belt buckle maybe—and there are signs of at least two previous fractures, his forearm and a rib. Maybe two or three years ago.'

'Had he been sexually assaulted?' asked Blizzard after a pause, his mind going back to the death of Danny Maddox at the hands of Albert Macklin two decades before.

'Not during the attack.'

'But before perhaps?'

'Yes,' nodded Reynolds, moving over to the sink and starting to wash his hands. 'Over several years.'

'Just what we need,' murmured Blizzard.

'Like that Maddox boy,' added Reynolds, looking up from the sink and fixing an intent stare on the chief inspector.

'What do you mean?' said Blizzard sharply.

'Danny Maddox was one of the last post-mortems conducted by my father before he retired,' said Reynolds. 'He said it was one of the worst examinations he had ever carried

41

out. This boy's body has similar signs.'

'Jesus,' breathed Colley, glancing at the detective inspector, who was biting his lower lip furiously.

'Looks to me,' said Reynolds, turning round and shaking his hands dry before reaching for a towel, 'like those stories might be true after all, gentlemen . . .'

CHAPTER SEVEN

The stories to which Reynolds alluded had been around for years. All cities have them, dark tales backed by very little evidence but gleefully perpetuated by the conspiracy theorists, including police officers and journalists, all of whom, in Blizzard's view, should have known better. The rumours, in the case of Hafton, claimed that a ring of extremely influential and well-connected men had been preying on teenaged boys for years, protected by a veil of secrecy which the police had found impossible to penetrate. Blizzard was one of the many detectives who had, over the years, sought the breakthrough whenever tantalizing snippets of information came to the fore.

On one level, sanctioning such inquiries was an easy decision for him to take, on the other it was fraught with political danger: police resources were increasingly stretched and burglaries, drugs and anti-social behaviour were high on the chief constable's agenda, making it difficult to tackle ephemeral cases like the conspiracy theory without running into trouble from the brass. Blizzard knew this because, having attended several briefings by the chief, it had been made clear that results were the be-all-and-end-all, the standard by which the force would be judged.

It was already becoming harder for senior officers to gain permission for large manpower-hungry operations which were, in Blizzard's view, important but did not—could not—guarantee results. He had been in trouble for speaking his mind over the issue on a number of occasions. Some said it was why his career would progress no further despite his achievements and experience.

Blizzard heard the whispers but hung on to the hope that progression within the service was down to ability rather than saying the right thing to the right people. On those occasions when he had discussed it with Ronald, his friend had described his view as naïve. If he were honest with himself, Blizzard knew the superintendent was right.

Nevertheless, the chief inspector, quietly backed by Ronald despite his reservations, had been running covert inquiries ever since he had taken over western CID four years previously. Only one other Abbey Road officer knew that they took place—David Colley. The inquiries never appeared on any timesheet records and no overtime was ever claimed for them. The brass knew nothing. But it was a frustrating business: every time the investigators seemed to be getting somewhere, doors slammed shut in their faces and potential witnesses clammed up. This was nothing new, though. Blizzard recalled, as he strode through the corridors of Abbey Road Police Station towards the press conference forty minutes after leaving the hospital, how other detectives had been intrigued by the same stories. And he knew that one of the witnesses who had slammed a door in police faces more than once was none other than Bob Maddox in the years following the death of his teenaged son.

Although Blizzard had only been a rookie uniformed officer in those days, he had heard the whispers in the corners of police stations which suggested that Danny Maddox was the victim of something much larger than a lone predator who had lured him to the canal bank. The rumours suggested that it was too convenient a story, that Bob Maddox was being paid to offer his son to the ring and that Macklin was somehow involved. Of course, it could have just been gossip, police stations are full of it, but Detective Chief Superintendent Dennis Barry, the lead officer in the inquiry into Danny's death, believed the stories. He confirmed as much to Blizzard years later when the younger man became one of Barry's detective sergeants in eastern division CID. According to Barry, when it was put to Macklin during interviews following his arrest, he simply shook his head and refused to comment, declining to implicate himself or anyone else. On one occasion, when Barry felt that Macklin was weakening, the prisoner had even collapsed and been taken to hospital, an illness which the detective had been convinced was faked. Over the years following Macklin's conviction, Barry made several visits to see him in prison to see if time had changed his mind, but the result was always the same. Whatever the truth behind the conspiracies, Dennis Barry went to his grave a disappointed man and Albert Macklin kept his silence and served his time without demur. No appeal, no attempt to plea bargain, no deals with the parole board. Nothing. Just silence.

What Blizzard would give, he thought, as he reached the door to the briefing room where the media were assembled, to know where Albert Macklin was now. Someone was bound to ask. He was about to push his way into the room when he was approached by a handsome, well-groomed, fresh-faced young man with immaculate wavy brown hair and wearing a smart grey suit and shiny shoes. Blizzard felt his hand going up to his loosened tie in the way it also did with the beautifully groomed

Colley—and cursed himself inwardly. What was it about modern officers that made them so damned smart, he thought?

'What you got?' he asked brusquely, irritated that the grinning officer had noticed the tiny gesture with the tie.

Detective Inspector Graham Ross, head of forensics, held up a small plastic bag containing the shards of red wood from Josh Holdsworth's battered skull.

'We think; he said, 'that they come from some kind of bat or something.'

'A bat?' asked the bemused detective.

'Best we can come up with,' shrugged Ross. 'Until you have the weap—'

'Sir,' came a breathless voice. Colley came running along the corridor towards them, his green anorak stained dark with the rain which had fallen consistently throughout the search of the canal bank that morning. The other detectives watched in fascination as the sergeant held up a plastic bag containing a crudely painted red and yellow baseball bat, one side of it splintered and blood-spattered.

'One of the lads found it three hundred metres from where Josh's body was found,' said Colley, catching his breath, 'hidden behind a fence.'

'It certainly fits,' nodded Ross.

'There's more,' said Colley, turning the bat round and letting them read the spidery black-painted letters on its side.

'Property of St Mary's Church,' breathed Blizzard, after peering closely at the words.

'I put a call in,' nodded Colley. 'Talked to one of the churchwardens. Apparently they have a sports equipment store for the youth fellowship.'

'Including baseball bats?'

'Including baseball bats,' and Colley's eyes gleamed. 'What do you make of that then?'

'It's certainly very interesting. Did you ask the churchwarden for their security camera pictures from the hostel last night?'

'They don't have any cameras.'

'Why not?'

'Apparently the church council said that the Lord would protect the place.'

'Perhaps he'd also like to fix their broken windows,' grunted Blizzard, pushing his way into the briefing room and surveying the reporters and television crews without much enthusiasm. 'Wish me luck!!'

As it was, the press conference went off without a hitch. Ronald answered most of the questions, as was his wont, and Blizzard, attuned as ever to what the media wanted even though he detested dealing with them, came up with one or two juicy quotes. The name Albert Macklin did surface in a question asked by the evening newspaper reporter the detectives had seen outside the hostel but Ronald simply brushed the enquiry aside, saying there was nothing to link the old jailbird with the teenager's death. Blizzard glanced briefly across the room at Ross and Colley when Ronald said that. After twenty minutes, the press conference broke up and Ronald started to give an interview to the local BBC television crew so Blizzard and Colley slipped out and headed for the front entrance, overtaken by a desire for a bacon sandwich from their favourite café in the small shopping precinct a few hundred metres from the police station, before resuming their inquiries.

'I want to talk to the vicar of St Mary's,' said Blizzard grimly, as they walked down the corridor, 'Because if Macklin got hold of that bat from the church, he has got a lot of explaining to do.'

'And what about Bob Maddox? Do we haul him in?'

'Yeah,' nodded the chief inspector, leading the way into the reception and out towards the front door. 'He's the most likely to have chucked that stone through the hostel window—that or his Brain of Britain son. What's more . . .'

But he did not have time to finish the sentence because as he and the sergeant pushed their way out of the front door of the station, they were assailed by a large crowd of people, shouting angrily and jabbing fingers towards them. At their head, as last time, was Margaret Hatton, her beige raincoat speckled with rain despite her black umbrella. Next to

48

her, was Bob Maddox, bull-necked as ever, his white T-shirt sodden as the rain teemed down, his jeans scruffy and tattered as always. The detectives noticed a number of other faces from the protest outside the church the night before.

'We'll nick Maddox later,' hissed Blizzard. 'If we do it here, it'll cause a riot.'

'Sounds sensible.'

'How many more?' snarled Maddox, lurching towards them. 'How many more is he going to kill, Chief Inspector?'

The brief lapse into grief and contrition of the night before had been replaced by rage and his face was twisted and ugly in a leer which showed his crooked, yellowing teeth. Behind him, other people, men and women and even one or two children, mirrored his fury, jeering and jabbing accusing fingers at them.

'We are doing everything in our power to . . .' began Blizzard, but he was drowned out by yells.

'If I get my hands on that bastard,' snarled Maddox, but Margaret Hatton silenced him with an elegant wave of a gloved hand.

'Enough, Bob.' She turned to the chief inspector, and said in that calm, modulated voice, that Blizzard would have found attractive in different circumstances, 'You can see the anger of these people, Mr Blizzard. We did warn you about Albert Macklin.'

'I don't need warning about him,' said Blizzard icily. 'Besides, there is no evidence to connect him with the tragic death of this young man.'

He was about to make further comment when he noted to his annoyance that the reporters and photographers were tumbling down the steps to capture the confrontation, and resolved to keep his thoughts to himself. He started to walk away when Margaret Hatton stopped him in his tracks, her voice tinted with steel.

'You do not know where he is, do you?'

'No, we do not,' admitted Blizzard uncomfortably, turning round to face her. 'But like I—'

'So you can not say that he did not kill this poor boy?'

'We are not ruling out anything.'

Ugly murmurs rippled through the crowd.

'Chief Inspector,' shouted the evening newspaper reporter, 'isn't it right that you were so concerned about Albert Macklin being back on the streets that on Friday you warned him off?'

'I don't intend to conduct my inquiries for the benefit of the media!' snapped Blizzard and, as the crowd jeered and hollered, he stalked off down the street, followed by press photographers and television crews, although they gave up after a few moments, their pictures safely in the can. Colley followed his boss. He would not like to be in the vicar's shoes at that moment, he thought.

CHAPTER EIGHT

It did not appear that the Reverend Henry Sanders was particularly keen about being in his shoes either. The vicar was not a relaxed man as he sat in his office at St Mary's, eying the two detectives nervously. Colley examined him with interest as the officers waited for the answer to their question. Not what you expected of a man of the cloth. He looked, thought Colley, like a man with all the cares of the world upon his bony shoulders rather than one filled with the joyful Christian message. A wiry, short man in his early fifties, Henry Sanders had thinning, greasy black hair, receding almost as they watched, and his forehead was criss-crossed with wrinkles and glistening with beads of sweat, which he dabbed occasionally with a white hand-kerchief. His eyes were dark and haunted and his lips seemed tremulous, almost, thought Colley, as if he were about to burst into tears at any moment. Here was a man in fear of something.

Quite why he should be so anxious was a bit of a mystery to Colley. Henry Sanders, he recalled, had arrived at the church less than a year before in what was seen as a plum posting. There had been plenty of positive press coverage with Sanders talking grandly about a mission to take the word of God into the community. St Mary's was regarded by many as a go-ahead progressive church and had been steadily increasing its congregation until several hundred people flocked—as it were—from all over the city, necessitating the introduction of an extra service, making three on a Sunday.

The image was helped by the sense of haven which the church presented. Built during the '60s, it stood behind a low, immaculately maintained white picket fence, within its own landscaped grounds, their tidy grassed areas and apple trees in stark contrast to the shabby side streets which surrounded them. For many, St Mary's was seen as a beacon in an area desperately in need of some form of salvation. The large green-roofed building was divided into three, the main church connected by a short corridor to a hall and a suite of offices, in one of which they now sat. Next to the offices was the hostel, linked by a connecting door.

The church itself was large and airy, unlike, thought Colley, so many of the gloomy ones he had visited. Not for personal reasons, mind: Colley had no truck with religion, something he shared with Blizzard. No, a sad fact of modern life was that churches were often broken into. But not St Mary's.

He recalled having only once been in St Mary's as part of a community forum some months previously—Blizzard had dropped out at the last moment and dragooned his sergeant—and noticing with some surprise that there were no pews, the worshippers sitting instead on chairs and that there was no pulpit, the vicar preaching from a lectern on a small raised stage in the middle of the church, surrounded on all sides by the congregation. And through it all, Christ looked down on the congregation from the huge stained glass window on which the detectives had commented when called to the protest by Margaret Hatton and her followers on Friday night.

Now it was Monday and, having arrived at St Mary's around lunchtime, Blizzard and Colley had crossed the church and stood once again for a moment and surveyed the window before walking on towards the offices. Something had made Colley look back and he was surprised to feel a slight shiver run down his spine, noticing for the first time that Christ's eyes seemed to follow them round the room. The sensation disturbed Colley: he had faced down armed robbers, drug dealers and murderers before, so why should a picture designed to depict a character representing peace and love alarm him? Blizzard, noticing the sergeant, had stopped and looked up at the picture as well, his eyes drawn as before to the tank in front of the cross on which stood the soldier in grey uniform pointing a gun. Mother Teresa surveyed the scene benignly.

'Still don't get it,' Blizzard said, with a shake of the head.

'No,' replied Colley, and dragged his eyes away, heartily wishing that Jesus would do the same.

They had found the vicar in his office. Through the glass panel in the door they saw him start when Colley knocked. Here, thought the sergeant now, as he sat and waited for the clergyman to answer, was a frightened man. And he wanted to know why. So did Blizzard.

'I am waiting,' said the chief inspector after a few moments, an edge to his voice.

'I have to be careful what I say,' muttered the vicar, wringing his hands.

'Not to me, you don't!' snapped Blizzard. 'In case you had forgotten, a teenage boy has had his skull beaten in with a baseball bat from your church storeroom. I ask again, how did it get into the hands of the killer?'

'I don't know,' murmured the wretched clergyman and he seemed close to tears. 'I really don't know.'

Blizzard glared at Sanders then changed tack with his questioning.

'Did you know that Albert Macklin was being cared for at your hostel?' he asked pointedly.

'Yes,' muttered the vicar, staring at the

floor, refusing to meet the detective's stare.

'It seems to me—' said Blizzard, but he was interrupted when the office door opened and in walked a tall young man, unannounced and without having knocked.

'That will be all,' he said dismissively, the smooth voice modulated and confident.

Colley watched Blizzard in anticipation. The chief inspector was a man who liked to be in control of situations and no one spoke to him like that. Or rather, no one spoke to him like that twice. Most people learned the error of their ways pretty quickly.

'Excuse me?' asked Blizzard icily, recovering his composure, but hardly trying to conceal his annoyance at the interruption.

'I said that the reverend has answered enough questions,' said the man.

'Says who?' asked Blizzard curtly.

'I,' said the young man, not extending a hand, 'am Edgar Rose-Harvey, the chairman of our church council. Any questions about this church should be addressed to me and not to Mr Sanders. And I demand to know what is happening here.'

Colley watched in increasing fascination as Blizzard glared at him. Edgar Rose-Harvey was an interesting character indeed. The sergeant reckoned he could not be more than twenty-five yet had the presence of someone twice his age. His brown hair was cut short, clean, without a strand out of place, his face was unblemished, lean and spotless, not a freckle, not a trace of acne, and his eyes were a deep piercing blue. A slim, athletic man, he was dressed entirely in black, black jacket, black polo-necked sweater, sharply pressed black trousers and shiny black shoes. The overall impression was of an extraordinary, charismatic young man in total possession of himself and the situation. Blizzard would not like that, thought Colley. Not one little bit.

He didn't.

'You are in no position to demand anything,' rasped Blizzard, getting swiftly to his feet and moving to stand within inches of him, glaring deep into his eyes. 'This is a murder investigation and nobody demands anything of me.'

They stared at each other for a moment or two. Colley could sense the battle of wills, the unwavering stares, the defiant postures. For a moment he wondered if the young man would try to front it out but after a few moments, he lowered his eyes, shrugged and sat down next to the vicar. Colley glanced at the clergyman and was surprised to see that he had started to tremble. It seemed, thought the sergeant, as if Henry Sanders was in fear of the newcomer.

'I apologize,' said Rose-Harvey, his voice, which smacked of an upper class private school education, remaining calm but less confrontational as he assessed the situation. 'I was forgetting myself. These are disturbing times, as I am sure you will appreciate, what with poor Joshua and David.'

'Too right they are,' said Blizzard through pursed lips. 'And this church is one of the things that disturbs me the most. I want some answers and I want them now.'

'Of course,' nodded the young man, the words sounding contrite.

Genuine deference to the detective or clever psychology, thought Colley? The effect of this imposing young man was something he had rarely experienced. There are some people in life who have that magnetic, mesmeric quality which means you cannot take your eyes off them. Edgar Rose-Harvey was one such man, thought the sergeant.

Blizzard was not feeling the same fascination. A man who jumped to conclusions much quicker than his younger colleague, the chief inspector had decided within seconds that he disliked Rose-Harvey and was determined to keep the ascendance in their confrontation. He, too, had noticed the effect that Rose-Harvey had on the vicar and he wanted to know what was going on.

'So how can I help you?' asked Rose-Harvey coolly.

Blizzard cursed inwardly. In the few seconds he had been assessing the young man, he had lost control of the situation again. Suddenly Rose-Harvey was asking the questions.

Reminding himself not to make the same

mistake again, Blizzard asked, 'Well, for a start, I want to know how a baseball bat from your church store ended up being used to stove in a young man's head?'

'Was the store locked?' asked Rose-Harvey, his voice harsh as he turned his attention to the quivering vicar.

'I . . . I think so,' replied the vicar uncertainly.

'I hope for your sake that it was,' said Rose-Harvey cruelly, 'because if it turns out that your mistake let someone get hold of that bat to kill this poor boy there will be some difficult questions for you to answer, Henry.'

The vicar seemed to cower back into his seat.

'And I want to know about Albert Macklin,' said Blizzard, pressing home the initiative. 'I have to say I am not happy that a man like him is being cared for at a place like this.'

'Meaning?'

'A lot of children use this church, Sunday school, Scouts, toddler groups.'

'Yes, but there are strict controls. And, as I am sure you are aware, social services approved our plans.'

'More fool them,' scowled Blizzard. 'Anyway, would Macklin have had access to the store?'

'Mr Macklin,' replied the young man, pointedly using the surname, 'may have had such access. We encourage our guests to use the church as part of their rehabilitation.'

'Guests!' exclaimed Blizzard. 'Macklin is a child-killer, dammit!'

'We hope,' said Rose-Harvey, his eyes assuming a dreamy, far-off expression as he gazed past them and out of the window at the apple trees gently swaying in the breeze, 'that the power of the Lord will shine light into the darkest recesses of their hearts. We see ourselves as the conduit through which that light can shine.'

'Spare me the mumbo jumbo.' said Blizzard curtly, unimpressed. 'Do you know where Macklin is now?'

'I am afraid not,' said Rose-Harvey, ignoring the snub, 'David Reed said he had gone to see relatives in Derby but we do not know where, I am afraid. How is dear David?' Again, the words should have sounded sincere but the tone of voice was not.

'He's got a headache,' grunted Blizzard.

'A somewhat uncharitable comment,' replied Rose-Harvey calmly. 'Now, will that be all? I do have things to attend to.'

Irritated by the attempt to get rid of them, Blizzard glared at him, nodded and left the room without another word. As Colley closed the door behind them, he saw that Edgar Rose-Harvey had started berating the vicar, jabbing a finger menacingly at the older man who, once again, seemed cowed and broken.

'What the hell has happened here?' asked

Blizzard, walking across the church.

They walked down the short passage into the church hall, a large, light room with large plain glass windows in the ceiling and shiny wooden floors. At one end stood a selection of children's buggies and bicycles, used by the toddler group every Monday and Thursday afternoon. Not far away was the door to the storeroom, painted red. The detectives walked across to examine it.

'Forensics are on their way to have a look,' said Colley, examining the lock to see if it had been forced. 'But it looks OK to me.'

'So whoever got hold of that bat had a key,' said Blizzard. 'Or could walk around the church without being questioned. Like Macklin.'

'I guess so,' nodded Colley. 'Mind, it could have been someone from the outside. I looked on the noticeboard as we came in, there are all sorts of clubs and groups that meet throughout the week. In fact—'

' 'Ere, what you doin'?' shouted a gruff voice, and they turned to see the caretaker storming across the hall towards them.

'It seems,' said Colley sardonically, 'that there is not much welcome from anyone in the house of the Lord this morning.'

'Too bloody right,' grunted Blizzard, holding up his warrant card at the caretaker, a grey-haired man in his sixties, wearing a brown overall jacket, paint-flecked trousers and clutching a mop. 'We are police officers.'

'I 'eard about the boy,' nodded the man, anger leaving him as suddenly as it had erupted, and shaking his head. 'Terrible thing.'

'Indeed,' said Blizzard, sensing that this was the first time they had encountered genuine sadness since they had walked into the church. 'Tell me, would Josh Holdsworth have come to this church?'

'Yeah, his mother is 'ere every Sunday, sometimes comes to all three services—and young Josh was in the Scouts. Lovely young lad, he really was.'

'And his father?' asked Colley. 'Did he come to the church?'

'Steve?' The caretaker shook his head vigorously, a long grey hair flopping over his left eye. 'Na, he ain't the type.'

'Type?' asked the sergeant.

'God-botherers.'

Colley suppressed a smile. It was not exactly the kind of response you expected from a church caretaker.

'Do I assume,' said Blizzard, 'that you do not have much time for churchfolk then?'

'Don't mind churchfolk,' said the old man, spitting out his next words as he nodded backwards towards the office, 'it's them people I don't like.'

'Who?' asked Colley.

'The new lot,' said the caretaker, the distaste in his voice undisguised. 'Rose-Harvey and his cronies. Came a few months ago and they've taken the flippin' church over.'

'Came? From where?' asked Colley.

The caretaker shrugged.

'Who knows? A dozen of them turned up at church one Sunday morning, next thing we know there's thirty or forty of the buggers. They got themselves on every committee and now they run the church. Most of the old 'uns have left. Can't be doin' with all them tambourines and happy-clappy stuff. Besides, anyone as disagrees gets the treatment.'

'The treatment?' asked Colley.

'Yeah, sent to Coventry. I don't come any more. It ain't for me.'

Blizzard had been listening with great interest.

'And what do they believe?' he asked.

'They say they believe every word of the Bible,' replied the caretaker, the hostility clear as he added vehemently. 'Then they opened up that hostel thing, brought in them perverts. It ain't right, that it ain't.'

'And the vicar?' asked Colley. 'Is he one of them?'

'Na.' The caretaker gave a hollow laugh. 'He'd only been 'ere a couple of months when they turned up and he 'ates 'em. Not that he would ever say owt, mind. He's frightened of them, if you ask me.'

'I can believe that,' nodded Colley.

'And what's more—'

But the caretaker got no further because a voice rang out.

'Hey!'

They turned to see Edgar Rose-Harvey, his face dark as thunder, glaring at the caretaker as he strode across the hall. It was the first time they had seen him lose control of his emotions.

'Get back to your work!' he yelled furiously at the caretaker. 'If anyone talks to the police it will be me, do you understand?'

The caretaker gave him a disrespectful leer, turned on his heel and scuttled from the hall.

'You hardly seem to have a Christian-like way with people,' said Blizzard pointedly, as the young man approached, his heels clicking on the shiny floor and reverberating around the empty hall.

'On the contrary,' said Edgar evenly. 'We are the true believers, Chief Inspector. We are the ones who carry the Lord's message into the world. It is our job to bring loving light into dark hearts. It is our mission.'

'Well, as long as it doesn't get in the way of my *mission*,' said Blizzard sharply, 'we will get on all right. But I warn you, Mr Rose-Harvey, if I discover that you and your people are somehow involved in all this, that hostel will be closed down that fast—'

'I do not appreciate being threatened. I, too, have powerful friends.'

'If you mean God—'

'Actually,' smiled Rose-Harvey, 'I was thinking of City Hall.'

'Just keep your nose out!' snapped Blizzard, and leaving the threat hanging in the air, he turned and stalked across the hall towards the main entrance.

'I sense pent-up anger in your chief inspector,' said Edgar Rose-Harvey sadly, watching the chief inspector go.

'Yeah, he gets like that when people get killed on his patch,' replied the sergeant coldly.

'He must find us difficult to understand,' smiled the young man. 'If only we could bring the Lord into his life . . .'

'He'd only arrest him,' said Colley, turning as he saw a forensics officer enter the room. 'Please make sure nobody touches that storeroom door until our people have done their work. The House of the Lord is ours for the next few hours.'

And with that he followed Blizzard into the car-park where the chief inspector was leaning on the roof of his car, looking up again at the large glass window.

'There is something very wrong here, David,' he said softly, turning troubled eyes on his colleague. 'Very, very wrong . . .'

'I'm inclined to agree,' nodded Colley, hesitating for a moment.

'What is it?' asked Blizzard, noticing the sergeant's confusion.

'It'll sound stupid.'

'No difference there then.'

'Thanks. OK, this may sound crazy and I know it's a church and all that, but I got a terrible feeling of evil in there.'

'Not like you to get over-sensitive,' said Blizzard, glancing curiously at his sergeant.

'I know . . . but that place gave me the creeps. And that Edgar Rose-Harvey guy . . .'

'There certainly doesn't seem to be much in the way of Christian spirit,' nodded Blizzard, unlocking his car door. 'Come on . . . a grieving mother awaits.'

CHAPTER NINE

More bizarre circumstances it would not be possible to imagine, thought Blizzard as the detectives sat uncomfortably in the Holdsworths' living-room and tried to conceal their amazement at what they were seeing. They were in a small terraced house some 200 metres from St Mary's. In all but one aspect, it was an unremarkable house; the living room was tidy and well polished with pale blue flowered wallpaper, a beige sofa and armchair, a dark wood sideboard on top of which was a fruit bowl laden with apples and pears and a small table on which rested a green telephone and a phone book. In the corner was a television. Nothing unusual except that the room was crammed full of religious items. Colley and Blizzard exchanged glances; this was weird. There were crucifixes on the mantelpiece, plastic models of a smiling Jesus on the sideboard and the walls were covered with Christian pictures, Jesus giving the sermon on the mount, Jesus at the Last Supper, Jesus on the Cross. Jesus, Jesus everywhere, thought Blizzard.

Then there was the couple: Marian and Steve Holdsworth were as different as people could be. She, probably aged no more than 45, a small mousy woman, dull brown hair in a bob, cheekbones high and bony, nose thin and prominent, eyes red and bloodshot but strangely featureless for all that, lips quivering slightly. Dressed in a yellow housecoat and plain brown skirt, she gave the impression of a woman to whom nothing had happened in her life . . . until now.

Steve Holdsworth was different. Several years younger than his wife, a rig worker, he was a large, muscular man, reminiscent in demeanour to Bob Maddox, with whom the detectives knew he had been friendly for many years. Indeed, they had once been arrested together after a late-night brawl at a city centre pub. His hair cropped short, his face flattened like a bulldog's, the eyes fierce, the mouth seemingly only one twist away from a leer, Holdsworth cut a daunting figure.

Dressed in jeans and a black T-shirt which showed off the well-defined pectorals and the six-pack stomach, he was a man who exuded power. The kind of power, thought Blizzard grimly, which could easily have inflicted the kind of scars and fractures which Peter Reynolds had discovered on the body of his son.

What was most remarkable, thought the chief inspector, was the dramatically different ways in which the husband and wife seemed to have reacted to the death of their child; she hardly able to speak, voice trembling when she did, so low the detectives were struggling to hear her as she sat, handkerchief grasped in hands, body seeming to crumple from time to time; he, thought Blizzard, as if a pigeon from the cree in the backyard had been lost, a father feigning a total lack of concern, the voice strong, the manner confident, almost dispassionate. You couldn't account for how people reacted to tragedy but Blizzard disliked him immediately, a dislike which had grown throughout the interview, the father answering every question, cutting rudely across his wife's replies every time.

'Can you tell me,' asked Blizzard after several minutes, looking deliberately at Marian Holdsworth, sitting next to her husband on the sofa, 'why your son might have been down on the canalside?'

'Shouldn't have been,' replied Steve gruffly,

as his wife opened her mouth to reply. 'Told him to steer clear of there. Too many bloody weirdos.'

'Please let your wife answer some of the questions,' said Blizzard. 'I know this is difficult for both of you but I have to get some idea of what your son was doing there.'

Steve Holdsworth made no attempt to hide his distaste at the suggestion that his wife be allowed to voice an opinion.

'Mrs Holdsworth?' prompted Colley.

'Joshua was a lovely boy,' blurted out Marian. 'Never gave us any bother.'

'Did he know a man called Albert Macklin?' asked Blizzard, as she started to sob again.

'Did that bastard kill my son,' demanded the father furiously, jumping to his feet, 'because if he did, I'll tear him limb fr—'

'We have no evidence to prove that Albert Macklin killed your son,' said Blizzard quickly.

'Bob says he did,' retorted Holdsworth.

'Bob Maddox, I take it?'

'Yeah, says death is too good for him.'

'And when did you talk to Bob Maddox about it?' asked Blizzard. 'You only arrived home an hour or so ago, surely?'

'Saw him for a quick pint at the club,' said Holdsworth.

The detectives stared at him in amazement.

'Before coming home?' asked Colley at length.

'Yeah, needed someone to talk to.'

68

'What about your wife, what about what she was going through?' exclaimed the sergeant, unable to conceal his revulsion.

'She don't talk to me no more,' said Holdsworth and gestured to the paintings adorning the walls. 'Talks to Jesus bloody Christ instead.'

'My faith sustains me,' said Marian Holdsworth, sitting up straight for the first time in the interview, voice suddenly strong, filled with purpose. 'If He has taken Joshua, it is for a purpose.'

Holdsworth snorted and Marian started to sob again, the vigour sucked from her by her husband's reaction.

'I think you attend St Mary's?' asked Blizzard.

'Yes, I do,' and she looked the detective straight in the eye. 'They are wonderful people. They talk with the voice of God. Joshua loved it . . .'

'Rubbish!' snorted her husband. 'He liked the Scouts, that was all. He didn't have time for all that happy-clappy shite.'

'He did!' exclaimed his wife vehemently, turning baleful eyes on him. 'It is just that you never saw it. You never saw anything!'

For an uncomfortable moment or two there was silence as husband and wife glared at each other then Marian's strength seemed to leave her again and she slumped back in the sofa, sobbing bitterly.

'Is there any reason why your son might have had a baseball bat with him?' asked Blizzard, once she had recovered herself.

'Baseball!' exclaimed the boy's father. 'T'aint a proper game. Josh liked football! I used to take him to the match when I were home.' And he stared at them proudly.

'What about the injuries we found on him?' asked the chief inspector. 'The pathologist suggested they stretched back years, fractures, scarring. How did your son get them?'

'Dunno,' shrugged Holdsworth, suddenly suspicious and guarded in his response.

'Mrs Holdsworth?' asked Blizzard.

For a moment it seemed as if she was about to say something but after a glance at her husband's fierce expression, she shook her head.

'He were a boy,' explained his father. 'Boys get bumps and scratches.'

'Hardly bumps and scratches,' said Blizzard archly. 'And the pathologist says he may have been sexually abused.'

Mrs Holdsworth stifled a sob and her husband looked away.

'Did you know about this?' asked Blizzard.

Neither replied. It was clear neither would. After a few moments of frustrated silence, Blizzard stood up and said pointedly, 'Thank you for your help. We'll leave you to your grief for now.'

'If there is anything we can do . . .' began

Colley.

His wife shot the sergeant a look which was half-gratitude, half pleading. A strange look. One that troubled the sergeant.

'We'll sort it ourselves, thank you,' said Holdsworth firmly, as the detectives reached the door.

'Don't go looking for Macklin,' warned Blizzard, jabbing a finger at him. 'The last thing we want is another murder.'

At this, Marian Holdsworth collapsed in tears.

'I'm sorry,' said Blizzard hurriedly, realizing that in his determination to increase the pressure on her husband he was also increasing the misery on the wife.

'Just leave,' she sobbed, turning her red-raw eyes on the detectives. 'Just leave!'

Outside the house, Blizzard and Colley stood in the street for a moment, both feeling drained by the experience which both had just gone through.

'What a bastard!' exclaimed Colley at length, once they had got into the car and were heading out of the street. 'What an absolute bastard!'

'Grief affects people in strange ways,' said Blizzard, but it did not sound convincing.

'Come on!' said Colley. 'He's a bastard and you know it.'

'Yeah, you're right,' nodded Blizzard, turning out onto the main road. 'Run me through what criminal records said about him again.'

'Well,' said Colley, producing out a computer print-out, 'all that guff about taking his son to the football? Holdsworth has got five convictions for football violence. Even attacked a bobby during trouble outside one match, put him in hospital for three days. His son was with him when it happened. He was nine at the time.'

'Any charges relating specifically to the kid, though?'

'Not official—but I talked to one of the uniformed lads—Geordie Baines—who remembered being called to the hospital three years ago when Josh was there with a broken arm. Kid wouldn't say how he got it and Geordie had to let the case drop. But I wouldn't put anything past our Mr Holdsworth. Not exactly the milk of human kindness, is he?'

'It curdled a long time ago,' sighed Blizzard, as he guided the car through the traffic. 'He's a nasty piece of work is Steve Holdsworth and it's interesting that he and Bob Maddox have already talked.'

'And before he went home to see his wife,' said Colley, appalled as he recalled the revelation.

'Like he said,' grunted Blizzard. 'She speaks to Jesus about it.'

'All that stuff was certainly spooky,' nodded

the sergeant. 'So what's our next move?'

'Well, our Mr Maddox becomes more and more interesting, does he not?' said Blizzard, then cursed as a small red car shot out of a side street in front of them, forcing the chief inspector to slam on the brakes and hurl profanities at the driver.

'Some people aren't safe to be let out,' muttered Colley, peering at the car as they pulled alongside it at the lights and shaking his head when he saw a little old lady with her eyes fixed straight ahead, knuckles glowing as white as her hair as she gripped the steering wheel.

'So,' said the sergeant, shaking his head again as the lights changed and Blizzard edged the vehicle forward, 'Do we nick Maddox now?'

'You know what,' said Blizzard, with a rare grin, 'before we do that, I think it's time we gave this God guy a tug . . . don't you? Does Paradise come under western division jurisdiction?'

'Not usually,' grunted Colley, visualizing the rough housing estates and shabby back streets in which he tended to spend most of his time.

Blizzard chuckled.

CHAPTER TEN

They found Bob Maddox drinking in a seedy pub down by the docks shortly after three that afternoon, after spending a couple of hours making calls on some of his associates at their favourite haunts. None of them professed to know where he was but, in the end, a veiled threat to a landlord that his liquour licence must be due for renewal elicited the information they were seeking and soon they were entering the gloom of the Harry's Arms. The pub was located on the corner of one of the many streets which had fallen into dereliction as the docks closed down during the latter decades of the twentieth century and business after business moved out. Dock Street had been untouched as yet by the investment which was transforming the nearby marina, with its glitzy nightspots and yachts the size of houses, and the Harry's Arms' neighbours were closed warehouses, all dirt-ingrained windows, rotting wooden doors and signs bearing the faded letters of once affluent fruit importers. Several of the buildings had the unmistakable signs of fire damage, having become playgrounds for drug-takers, glue-sniffers and teenaged arsonists.

Once, there had been four pubs in Dock Street, all raucous nights, lewd behaviour and violent seamen's brawls which spilled out onto the street but which were always dealt with by the drinkers without police intervention, the badly injured spirited away into the night to be patched up to fight another day. Sometimes they were never seen again. Now, the Harry's Arms was the only survivor of those days. It had not always been like that. Dock Street was once one of the busiest places in the city, lined with chandlers' offices, sail-makers and fruit suppliers, all serving the mighty ships that began their journeys of exploration at Hafton. Those had been glorious days in the life of the city, heady days when businessmen became rich beyond their wildest dreams and young men volunteered eagerly for the adventure of a life at sea, their minds filled with romantic notions until they discovered the reality of life on the ocean wave. Many did not come back, falling victim to scurvy and the other diseases which stalked the decks of the ships. Yet, some made their fortunes and one such man was Harry Arbuthnot.

The son of a local seventeenth-century merchant, he sailed the world on his father's ships and rose to become a captain and one of the greatest adventurers in the city's history before perishing, somewhat romantically, at the hands of irate natives on a far flung Caribbean shoreline. The good burghers of Hafton erected a statue of him in the main city square—still there, much beloved by pigeons and not cleaned for years—and the Harry's Arms was re-named in his honour shortly after his death at the age of 36. Today, the pub was a sad and neglected testimony to his faded memory, those windows not boarded up lined with grime, the paintwork peeling on the sills and the cracks and blisters on its sign making the name and face of the seaman virtually indecipherable.

The Harry's Arms was not actually in the western division—it was part of the city centre beat—but was well known to Blizzard and Colley as a hang-out for many of their villains. Everyone from drug dealers to burglars came to the Harry's Arms to drink long into the afternoon and hatch their plots amid the stale smell of decay. The pub, it was said, sold the cheapest clock radios in the city but whenever the police raided, they had somehow been spirited away like those injured seventeenth-century brawlers.

When the detectives pushed their way into the lounge, it was dark as usual, partly because of the fug of smoke from cigarettes and partly because the walls were covered with a dark wallpaper which might have once been red. Adding to the oppressive atmosphere was a carpet stained brown from decades of filth and trodden-in fag-ash, to which the officers' shoes stuck as they walked towards the bar. The detectives were acutely aware of the hostile expressions of the few men gathered round the tables, drinking their pints and talking in low conspiratorial voices.

Bob Maddox was sitting at the bar, deep in conversation with a man they recognized as an armed robber who had recently been released from Hafton Prison, a huge, skinhead Irishman known for his violent behaviour and short fuse.

'Do you think we need to call for back-up?' whispered Colley, displaying unaccustomed nervousness.

'No need,' replied Blizzard confidently. 'Me and Pat go back a long way. He'll give us no trouble.'

Maddox swung round on his stool and eyed the detectives suspiciously. Big Pat glowered at them but did nothing. Blizzard nodded at him and without a word the Irishman slunk away to join a group of the drinkers in the corner.

'Time for a chat, Bob,' said Blizzard calmly.

'I ain't got nothing to do with Josh's death,' said Maddox defiantly.

'That may be so, but I am here about David Reed.'

'Who's he?'

'The young man at the hostel—someone chucked a rock through the window last night.'

'What's that got to do with me?'

'That's what I would like to know,' said Blizzard coolly. 'Where were you last night, Bob?'

'That's easy,' said Maddox. 'I was at home.'

'Can anyone verify that?' asked the chief inspector.

'The missus and that Margaret Hatton woman.'

'She seems to be cropping up like a bad penny,' murmured Blizzard. 'Now, pray what was she doing at your house, may I ask? Surely you weren't having a dinner party? You haven't been making vol-au-vents again, have you, Bob? And I hear your canapés are sensational.'

'We were talking about the hostel,' retorted Maddox, bridling at the mocking tone in the detective's voice. 'We want it closed down and she is going to help us. She were at our house until late. You ask her.'

'We will. Are you sure you didn't nip out for a few minutes to throw that rock?' asked Colley, rapidly regaining his confidence.

'Na. Margaret says we ain't going to gain owt if we attack folks.'

'Well, she's right there,' nodded Blizzard, eying Maddox keenly but finding no sign that he was lying.

'Listen,' said Maddox, leaning forward earnestly. 'I ain't no angel, Mr Blizzard—'

'You can say that again.'

'But I ain't so stupid as to do something like that.'

'Someone did,' pointed out Colley. 'And you did rush the building on Friday night, remember?'

'Yeah, I know, but it weren't me that threw that stone. Honest. Margaret says that is playing right into their hands.'

'Whose hands?' asked the chief inspector.

'Eh?'

'Whose hands?' repeated Blizzard.

'She didn't say. But it is.'

Blizzard gave a mirthless smile. 'OK, Bob,' he said. 'I'll take your word for it. But any more trouble and I'll be back—do you understand?'

The stare was icy, daring Maddox to challenge the statement. He didn't but nodded meekly.

'One more thing,' said the chief inspector. 'What did you and Steve Holdsworth talk about when he got back from the rig?'

'T'ain't none of anyone's business,' said Maddox gruffly, clearly startled that they knew about the conversation.

'I think it is.'

'You've met his wife,' shrugged Maddox. 'He needed someone to talk to. What we talked about was between me and 'im.'

Blizzard nodded—he'd find out one way or another—and the detectives headed for the door, shoes still sticking to the carpet. When they reached it, Blizzard paused with his hand resting on the handle and looked slowly around the room, taking in the familiar faces sitting at the tables.

'Gentlemen,' he said coldly, 'it's been an

absolute pleasure.'

And he pushed his way out into the drizzle of the afternoon, smiling as he ignored the baleful stares which followed him.

CHAPTER ELEVEN

It was no ordinary gathering that evening at Arthur Ronald's large detached home in an exclusive gated housing complex in one of the plush villages on the western edge of the city. Officially it was not even taking place. Sitting in his favourite armchair in his spacious cream-carpeted lounge, surrounded by his beloved French Impressionist prints and exotic ornaments gleaned from holidays around the world, the detective chief superintendent eyed the four men affectionately.

You couldn't get a more varied bunch, he reflected. Contrasting individuals they might be but they were united in their burning desire to crack one of the most baffling mysteries in the city's modern history. The other characteristic that bonded them together was their loyalty to each other. These, mused Ronald, were men with whom he would trust his life; his professional life was already in their hands anyway because were their activities—and his blessing for them—to be uncovered by the top brass, his career would almost certainly be curtailed. They wouldn't appreciate a senior officer sanctioning covert inquiries without their knowledge. He could say goodbye to any further promotions.

First of all there was John Blizzard, calm as ever, slumped comfortably in an armchair, flicking through his small blue notebook as he composed his thoughts. He still wore his dark suit from work, having only just left Abbey Road shortly before nine after an exhausting day. Next to him was Colley, the younger man eying Ronald intently as he waited for the meeting to start. He seemed slightly troubled, thought Ronald, the eyes tired and strained, the usual cheerfulness banished for the time being. It was always like this when you worked on child murders, thought the superintendent. You never got used to it. He could still clearly see the bodies of the children whose deaths he had investigated down the years. Those images never left you.

Beside the sergeant, on one end of a cream sofa, sat an officer in his early fifties, hair almost grey now, thinning and cut short, face chiselled and slightly pock-marked, eyes deep and dark, the face bearing a world-weary expression from seeing too much evil. He was dressed in an ill-fitting navy-blue suit, the tie having been removed and shoved into his jacket pocket the moment he arrived at the house. This was Detective Sergeant Max Randall, a veteran who had worked with

81

Ronald over at the eastern division, where he was still based despite attempts to entice him away. Promotion and a move to pastures new had been offered several times but Randall had always turned it down. Not for him, he always said, in that gravelly voice of his.

Next to him sat the final member of the gathering. No suit here. Alex Mather, a man in his late twenties, was a vice squad detective officer who spent much of his time working undercover. Slim with light brown hair which was still wet, the officer having popped back to his flat to take a quick shower in deference to his colleagues, he was dressed in scuffed jeans and black T-shirt. Despite the shower, his lean face remained unshaven and his eyes were alert, keenly surveying each officer, his overall demeanour that of a man who spent his life in difficult situations and was used to constantly watching his back. Even among trusted friends, he found it difficult to relax entirely.

Two very different men, thought Ronald, but joined together by one fact, that both had been divorced through the pressures of the job, something they shared with John Blizzard. Randall's wife had taken their two teenaged sons away several years before, arguing that he spent more time at the police station and the nearby pub than at home. Mather's wife had similarly taken their baby daughter away two years before, unable to cope any more with his erratic lifestyle and the way he would turn up at strange times of night and day but never explain where he had been. His little daughter had even cried in terror when he walked in one night, the detective having grown a straggly beard in the time he had been away. It proved the final straw and his wife left to stay with her mother. Six months later they were divorced and although she let him see his daughter regularly, and had briefly held out hope of a reconciliation, the gesture had not stopped Mather doing the undercover work. Like all the men in the room, he was driven, and by this inquiry more than any other.

On the glass coffee table in front of them was a selection of foil take-away curry containers with the remainders of a meal which had been delivered some time before. Each time they met, they abided by their golden rule: no one talked business until the food had been eaten. Frankly, none of them wanted to talk at first, having tucked into the meal with gusto, each man having been summoned to Ronald's house after a busy day. Blizzard and Colley had been working the Josh Holdsworth case, ensuring that house-to-house inquiries were made near the canal, co-ordinating the team of twenty detectives who were working on the case. But their efforts had turned up little fresh evidence, frustrating for Blizzard and his sergeant, who had hoped for more, particularly since the press office was being bombarded with media inquiries about the case. The media interest, it seemed, had been orchestrated by Margaret Hatton, who was showing an innate ability to court journalists by feeding them tit-bits of information and coming up with exactly the right soundbite. She would not, it seemed, cease her activities until Albert Macklin was arrested and charged with the murder of Josh Holdsworth.

To counter her negative comments about the police, Blizzard had been persuaded by Ronald and the press office to give several grudging interviews to television, radio and newspaper reporters, which seemed to have slowed down the frenzy a touch. But the officers knew it would only be temporary and that they would be clamouring for more in the morning. Adding to their frustration with Margaret Hatton was her confirmation of Bob Maddox's alibi for the night David Reed was attacked.

Max Randall, over at the eastern division, had been dealing with a particularly nasty rape and had derived great satisfaction from making an arrest late that afternoon; Alex Mather had been working an inquiry into a violent pimp on one of the city's housing estates, dangerous undercover work in an investigation which was close to a successful resolution after three months in which he had hardly seen his home. Although Randall and Mather were not directly involved in the inquiry into Josh Holdsworth's death, neither had been surprised to receive the call from Arthur Ronald inviting them to his home that evening. Indeed, they had expected it. These men were the team behind Operation Keeper. Not that anyone would recognize the name. It was not an official operation and the codeword proved useful shorthand for communicating with each other. It was Colley, ever impish, who had suggested the name because they wanted something which reflected the nature of their work but which would be difficult, if not impossible, to fathom should anyone overhear them use the phrase. David Icke, the sergeant had pointed out, was a great conspiracy theorist and also once played in goal for Coventry City. So Operation Keeper it was.

The operation had been running covertly ever since Blizzard took up his posting at the western division and was the inquiry, most of it conducted in off-duty hours, into the rumours of a sex ring operating in the city. Alex Mather was there because, as a vice squad officer, he had immense knowledge of the seedier side of the city's life, and Max Randall was chosen because he had worked extensively with Ronald and Blizzard when they were based in the eastern division and had, over the years, become convinced that there was some truth to the rumours. People told Randall things and he was more sure than ever that Albert

Macklin was involved and that Danny Maddox had been its first victim, killed twenty years ago, he speculated, because he had been about to open his mouth to tell everything he knew. Many of Randall's theories had been formed during conversations with his great friend Dennis Barry, the detective who had investigated Danny Maddox's death and with whom the sergeant had worked for many years. They had been confirmed by tantalizing information from contacts on the ground, but never enough to warrant a formal investigation, will-o'-the-wisp snippets which evaporated almost as soon as they were conveyed. And, given that the team agreed they only had one shot at breaking open the ring and that if it was done, it had to be done right, they simply could not take the risk of going in without enough evidence. Besides, at the moment they only knew one or two of the foot-soldiers like Macklin, no one knew the identity of the big players.

Ronald had agreed to let the operation run covertly because, squeezed ever more to cut costs and limit overtime, he knew senior officers would not sanction expenditure on what they regarded as an urban myth. But also because he suspected there was an element of truth to the rumours. Now, he leaned back, licked his fingers of curry sauce and reached for the glass of white wine on the table beside his chair.

'Excellent meal, they do a truly wonderful biryani,' he said, looking with a crestfallen expression at the empty foil containers. 'I could eat it again.'

'Indeed,' grinned Mather. 'Seem to have forgotten to eat anything this year.'

Blizzard and Colley nodded: a snatched ham sandwich on the run had been just about all they had eaten for the past eight hours. Randall said nothing; nobody had seen him eat anything since 1987 anyway—and even then it was a bag of crisps with his pint.

'So,' said Ronald, putting down his glass. 'Is Keeper a separate inquiry, or is Josh Holdsworth's death wrapped up in it somehow? Where are we, John?'

Blizzard took a sip from his can of lager.

'Well,' he said, 'it has all the hallmarks of another Danny Maddox. The kid had been abused over a long period of time.'

'By his dad?'

'Don't know. We are doing some tests.'

'What did the dad say?' asked Mather.

'Didn't seem to care that his son was dead. Just acted like it was a problem out of the way, didn't he, Dave?'

'Yeah,' nodded Colley. 'The wife was in bits but Holdsworth just bad-mouthed the kid.'

'Maybe it is the same inquiry,' said Randall. 'Dennis Barry always reckoned Danny Maddox was killed to stop him blabbing. Perhaps it was the same with Josh. Maybe

87

Macklin does their dirty work for them.'

'Alex?' asked Ronald.

'It doesn't make sense,' replied Mather, his voice light and lilting, with a trace of his Scottish roots.

'Meaning?' said the superintendent.

'Why wait for Macklin to get out? There's plenty of meat-heads would be happy do it if the price was right. They didn't have to wait for chummy to come out to play.'

'Na, I fancy Macklin for this,' growled Randall. 'Too much of a coincidence. Guy comes out, kid is dead within forty-eight hours—and at the same place with the same m.o. He's got to be your man, John, got to be.'

'To shut him up?' asked Ronald, taking another sip of wine. 'Bye, that's a nice drop.'

'Amazing what you can get at Threshers for £2.99,' said Randall slyly.

'It certainly wasn't £2.99!' exclaimed Ronald.

The other officers grinned; if there was one thing Arthur Ronald prized above all others, it was his reputation as a wine aficionado and he and his wife spent plenty of money indulging their passion, often taking their children to wine regions of France and Italy for their holidays. Ronald noticed the smiles and raised his eyes to the ceiling in mock exasperation.

'To answer your question,' said Randall, suddenly serious again and pausing to think, respectfully allowed to collect his thoughts by his colleagues, 'I am sure Bob Maddox is involved in the ring . . . I have heard his name mentioned . . . he's a foot soldier probably, nothing more. But I never heard anyone mention Steve Holdsworth. Never.'

'But Holdsworth admitted he talked to Bob Maddox even before he went home to his wife,' pointed out Colley. 'That's got to mean something, surely? Maybe Maddox is tied up in all this.'

'I'm not saying he isn't,' nodded Randall. 'But I still fancy Macklin for this.'

'What about the church?' asked Ronald. 'Hasn't there been whispers about a church being involved, Max? Could it be St Mary's?'

'There has been mention,' nodded Randall, 'but nothing definite. Like always, people let something slip then clam up. They're scared of something, that's for sure.'

'So where do we go now, gentlemen?' asked Ronald, lifting the wine bottle and offering it round. 'If I make this official, the brass—'

'Hang on,' said Blizzard wickedly, declining the wine and heading for the kitchen, 'you are the brass!'

The others laughed. Ronald took the jest in good part.

'Whatever,' he said. 'Like I was saying before I was so rudely I interrupted by my junior officer . . .'

More chuckles.

'I heard that,' said Blizzard's disembodied

89

voice, as he reached into the fridge for another can of lager.

Ronald smiled then continued in a sombre voice, 'If I suddenly announce to the chief constable that we think that Josh Holdsworth's death is linked to the ring, I know what he'll say: the budget is half a million short, I can't even get sanction for more paperclips; and the chief will demand evidence—and I wouldn't blame him. And we don't have evidence, do we, gentlemen?'

'Not really,' admitted Blizzard, returning to sit down in his armchair and crack open the can.

'So,' concluded Ronald, 'there is no way I can get extra manpower to investigate our theories without further evidence—unless we can get something to tie it in with the death of Josh Holdsworth.'

He glanced at Mather and Randall.

'And unfortunately, there is no way I can swing it for either of you two to be seconded onto the murder inquiry. You're needed elsewhere.'

They nodded, Randall adding mischeviously, with a glance at Blizzard, 'Pity, because John does need an experienced hand to make sure it is being run right.'

Blizzard gave him a mock withering look; he and Randall went back a long time.

'So we keep our suspicions to ourselves for the moment, do we?' asked Mather.

'As before,' nodded Ronald.

'I think that is the only way to play this,' nodded Randall, lowering his voice conspiratorially. 'If we are right and there are powerful people involved, the last thing we want is word getting out in the police that—'

'Hang on,' said Ronald sharply. 'Are you suggesting that a senior police officer could be involved because if you are—'

'Come on,' protested Randall. 'I am only saying what we have all been thinking the last four years. Isn't that right, John?'

And he fixed his gaze on Blizzard, who took another sip from his can of lager.

'Maybe,' he said, shrugging in a non-committal way. 'Maybe.'

'Well, this had better not go outside these four walls,' said Ronald vehemently. 'And I hope you're wrong about one of our own, Max.'

No one in the room thought he sounded convinced.

'So do I,' replied Randall and he looked at each one of them in turn. 'So do I . . .'

CHAPTER TWELVE

Tuesday morning dawned bright and sunny and Blizzard's mood brightened with it. As he drove in from his home in the small village of Haltby, appreciating the dusting of dew on the bare fields, he allowed himself the first genuine smile since he had been asked to confront Albert Macklin five days before. The sunshine helped; Blizzard had long suspected that he was one of those people who were badly affected by the weather. This theory had come about because he had sensed a distinct change in his character over the years and could not work out if it was simply part of the ageing process—it seemed to him that police officers aged quicker than others—or a change in his approach to life. As a young, idealistic rookie, he had been a positive individual, keen to see the good side of life in everyone. But as the years passed, he experienced darker moods and those darker moods tended to be more profound in the winter months.

He had even—although he detested doctors—sought medical opinion from his GP as to whether he suffered from SAD—was one of those people in whom dark winter months brought about depression. His GP, a sallow, equally SAD man in his late fifties, had seemed monumentally uninterested in the case and had offered to prescribe Blizzard some anti-depressants and tablets to help him sleep at night. Blizzard had declined. Detectives need clear heads, he had retorted. His doctor had simply shrugged.

However, sleep was a problem and Blizzard

yawned several times as he drove into the western edge of the city, passing through wide tree-lined avenues where could be found the biggest, most exclusive houses in town. This was where the money was: every house had a long drive, was partly obscured from the road by mature trees and every other home had a swimming pool. It always amused Blizzard to see who owned the houses: most were legitimate people, company executives, self-made businessmen and the like but some, he knew but could not prove, were into crime: men who covered their tracks but made a handsome profit from drugs. Just the kind of people, thought Blizzard glumly, who could be involved in the sex ring. Untouchable. Or so it seemed to him and not surprisingly, with the death of Josh Holdsworth preying on his mind, his bad dreams had started again.

Blizzard had experienced increasing sleep problems in the years since his wife had left him. They might not have got on in the later years but it was nice to roll over to someone in the morning. Whenever he was investigating particularly troubling crimes, Blizzard tended to have bad dreams and last night had been no exception, the detective having woken up three or four times because he kept seeing the teenager's crumpled body on the canal bank. As he drove, his mood turned darker again and he cursed himself for failing to control his mind.

When he pulled into the car park behind Abbey Road Police Station, however, there was better news, which cheered him up considerably. Colley had been watching out of the CID office window and, on seeing the car pull up, walked out, pulling on his anorak.

'Where you off to?' asked Blizzard, getting out of the car.

'Something you might be interested in,' replied the sergeant. 'A woman saw you appealing for help on the telly last night and rang the incident room. Reckons she saw someone looking like Albert Macklin hanging around the canal at the time Josh was killed.'

'Really?' said Blizzard with interest, as the two men swung themselves into the vehicle.

'Yes,' and Colley gave that mischievous look of his as Blizzard backed the car out of its parking space, 'and she also said you seemed like a nice-looking man. You might be in there, boss.'

'And how old is she?' asked Blizzard suspiciously, well used by now to his sergeant's humour.

'Seventy-three.'

Colley was still grinning as they pulled up outside the old people's sheltered complex fifteen minutes later. Blizzard, also enjoying the joke, had played along, occasionally sighing and shaking his head or shooting sour looks at the chortling sergeant. Five minutes later, they were sitting in the small, tidy flat of

Agnes Proud, surrounded by the trinkets which chronicled her life, photographs of her dead husband and her beaming grandchildren, cat ornaments and a couple of cheap and nasty, faded model camels brought back from a holiday to Tunisia many years before.

'Mrs Proud,' said Colley, trying but failing to imagine her on a camel as he sat down and accepted the cup of tea and saucer, 'can you go through again what you saw on Sunday?'

'Biscuit?' she asked, offering round a plate of custard creams. 'You young men have got to keep your strength up.'

'Er no, thanks,' said Colley. 'Sunday afternoon, Mrs Proud?'

'Well,' she said, voice firm and definite, sitting down in a battered old armchair and reaching for a biscuit. 'It was about three o'clock and I was having a walk along the canal: I like to have a walk on a Sunday, keeps my old joints in working order.'

Colley nodded: he liked her instantly and sensed that, if required, she would be an excellent witness.

'Then what did you see?' he asked.

'I saw an oldish-man walking along the path towards me.'

'What was he wearing?'

'A long brown raincoat—it seemed new—and a scruffy brown suit. Didn't really seem to fit him, seemed a bit baggy and the lapels were frayed. It was definitely an old suit, you don't see that design these days.' She smiled. 'I worked in a clothes shop for many years. You look for these things straight away.'

The detectives exchanged glances: apart from the new raincoat, which he could have bought on release, she was describing the clothes which Albert Macklin had been wearing when they saw him outside the prison on Friday morning.

'What was his face like?' asked Colley.

'No need for a description,' said Agnes confidently. 'It was Albie Macklin all right.'

'But how do you know?' pressed Colley. 'The picture in the media was taken eighteen years ago when he was sent to prison. He has changed a lot since then.'

'Not that much,' and she smiled sadly. 'I have known Albie for many years. We went to school together. He was a wrong 'un then. After we left school, I often used to see him around town—when he wasn't in prison. You don't think he did this, do you?'

And she turned anxious eyes on the detectives. Blizzard shrugged.

'I don't know what to think,' he said. 'I do hope not.'

'That's what I said to the vicar,' she nodded.

'Henry Sanders?'

'Yes, such a nice man.'

'You go to St Mary's then?' asked Colley.

'Not any more,' and she seemed saddened for a moment. 'When those young people moved in they didn't seem to want old fuddy duddies like me. I go to St Columba's now.'

'So how did you see the vicar?' asked Blizzard.

'Oh, he was down by the canal as well. I saw him a few minutes after I saw Albie. He was walking down the path towards the city centre. He seemed in a hurry.'

The detectives looked at each other sharply.

'Let me get this right,' said Blizzard slowly. 'Henry Sanders was on the towpath at the same time as you saw Albie?'

'Yes, we stopped for a chat but he didn't really want to talk,' she said, then suddenly realized the import of what she saying and clapped a hand to her mouth, eyes wide with horror. 'Oh, but surely you don't think . . . ?'

'It's probably coincidence,' said Blizzard hurriedly, wary of giving anything away. 'I am sure there is a perfectly innocent explanation.'

Agnes relaxed. 'I am sure there is,' she said confidently 'Such a nice man—but always so worried. I blame those strange young people at the church.'

The detectives thanked her, declined another cup of tea, made their excuses and left. Outside they walked to the car in silence. It was not until they reached it that Colley spoke.

'What do you think?'

'I don't know what to think,' said Blizzard, leaning on the car roof and looking across at his sergeant. 'I didn't miss anything, the vicar did not mention that he was down on the towpath did he?'

'Definitely not,' said Colley.

'Thought so. I think we had better pay him another visit, don't you?'

'Certainly do. Oh, while I remember, any chance I can get away six-thirtyish tonight?'

'Jay want to take you to Sainsbury's?' said Blizzard slyly, unlocking the door.

'Not quite!' grinned Colley. 'It's training. We've got that floodlit pitch over on Bernwell Avenue. It's us against Broughton at the weekend; can't lose that one.'

Blizzard nodded. His sergeant was a keen rugby player and always did his best to make sure he played in as many matches for the divisional team as possible. He could even lay claim to having solved a crime while scrumming down. Not that the solution came to him in a flash of inspiration while binding with a sweaty sergeant from another division, rather that, as he bent down, he glanced back through the hooker's legs and glimpsed a missing suspect standing on the touchline. Within seconds, the terrified man had been arrested, the custody sergeant flummoxed when fifteen western division officers tried to claim the collar.

The chief inspector encouraged his rugby. The job was tough, he believed, and every officer needed a release. His was as far from the sporting field as it was possible to imagine. John Blizzard, feared by villains, admired as a tough operator by colleagues and respected, although sometimes grudgingly, by the brass, was a railway enthusiast and had for several years been one of a number of volunteers working to restore a steam locomotive, the Silver Flyer. When things got difficult and he needed time to think, John Blizzard would head for the shed in which she was housed, spending hours lovingly working up to his elbows in muck and grease while his mind sorted things out. More than one crime had been solved while sitting beside the Silver Flyer on a chilly winter's evening, warming himself by the small heater, sipping a cup of tea and staring into thin air. And with a lot of thinking to do on this occasion, Blizzard was quite hoping to get a break himself and pop down the shed that evening.

Blizzard knew that the rugby match against Broughton was a big one. Broughton was a small town twenty miles away and the rivalry between the two divisions had always been fierce, partly because a number of the city officers had moved over into senior positions at Broughton and also because of the long-standing strong sporting links between the two.

'Yeah,' nodded Blizzard. 'You can get away OK. To be truthful, I was going to pop in on the Old Lady.'

Colley shook his head. 'You and that bloody

train . . . ?'

'Locomotive,' said Blizzard archly. 'I hate it when people get that wrong. Locomotives pull trains. It's not difficult to understand.'

'Whatever,' grinned Colley, doing up his seatbelt as Blizzard started the engine. 'Whatever . . .'

CHAPTER THIRTEEN

The Lord may move in mysterious ways, remarked Blizzard shortly after four that afternoon, but they were nothing compared to the bewildering movements of the vicar. The chief inspector and Colley were sitting in Blizzard's office at Abbey Road Police Station sifting through reports of what had been achieved during the day. Of Henry Sanders there was no sign at all. Checks had revealed that all the hostel residents, apart from Macklin, could account for their whereabouts when Josh Holdsworth was killed but by now, the detectives' focus had switched to someone within the church, someone who had access to the storeroom, and their attention was firmly focused on the vicar, with the sighting of him on the canal bank allied to his disturbed expressions and anxious body language when they had first questioned him.

Having identified tracking down the

reverend as their top priority, the detectives had made three visits to St Mary's, twice to be met by the caretaker who said the clergyman had left the church around lunchtime, the third by Edgar Rose-Harvey, cool and unruffled as ever, who said he had no idea where the vicar was. His body language suggested he did not care either. As they left the church the third time, shortly before three 3.30, they had been perturbed to see a group of protestors standing nearby with placards demanding that the hostel be closed. At their head, as ever, was Margaret Hatton, giving interviews to a national news television crew, pointing at the hostel from time to time. Blizzard and Colley had scuttled away before the television crew saw them. Blizzard had been interested to note that there was no sign of Bob Maddox in the group of protestors. Maddox had certainly made himself scarce since their meeting in the pub. Not surprising, since Detective Sergeant Tulley had been tasked to find out more about his movements in the hours before the attack on the hostel which had left David Reed seriously ill in hospital. Blizzard had ordered him to do it in a high profile way to increase the pressure on Maddox.

Other officers had also been reporting in during the day, one of the reasons Blizzard had returned to the police station. Now, he was sitting at his desk, tipping backwards on his chair as usual, sipping from a steaming mug of tea and flicking through sheafs of paper. Colley was sitting on the other side of the desk, reading another report and occasionally reaching out for his mug of tea.

'We're getting nowhere fast,' remarked Blizzard at length, tossing the reports down onto the desk, which was its usual untidy self, strewn with briefing papers from headquarters which he was supposed to have read but had studiously ignored for several days.

'Yeah,' nodded Colley, holding up the report he had been reading. 'Derby police are having no luck with Albert Macklin. They checked out a few leads but they turned out to be mistaken identity.'

'They won't find him,' said Blizzard confidently, grounding his chair. 'I reckon he's still here.'

'Maybe,' said Colley, then adding curiously, 'What do you make of Margaret Hatton?'

'A smart cookie.'

'Too smart.'

'Meaning?' asked the chief inspector, eying his sergeant intently.

'Well, she's playing a game, isn't she? All those media interviews. She seems to like getting her face on the telly and in the papers. You can't move without seeing her. And she was on the radio news this afternoon saying we should have arrested Macklin the moment he got out.'

'Yeah, but on what charge?'

'Said it didn't matter, society had to be protected from men like that etc etc.'

'She's certainly stirring it up,' acknowledged Blizzard, getting to his feet and glancing at the clock on the office wall. 'Anyway, I seem to recall you saying you wanted to practise knocking seven shades out of our esteemed colleagues at Broughton so get on with you.'

'God, I'd forgotten that!' exclaimed Colley, glancing at his watch and reaching for his anorak. 'Thanks for reminding me.'

'See you tomorrow,' smiled Blizzard, as the sergeant rushed out of the room.

It was an affectionate smile: he liked David Colley. The sergeant was loyal, straightforward and honest but prepared to speak his mind if he thought his boss was wrong. Blizzard appreciated that in a sergeant; it was why he had recommended him for promotion from detective constable. Still thinking about Colley, Blizzard pulled on his jacket, wandered up to front office to tell them where he was and headed out into the night. Half an hour later, he was unlocking the padlock to a corrugated-iron engine shed on wasteland beyond the complex of railway lines at the edge of the city centre. The area had been designated for a regeneration scheme but plans for a supermarket had been withdrawn when subsidence, the legacy of the area's industrial past, was discovered and the cost of

103

remedial work rocketed. Since then, the site had been left to slip gently into dereliction. Which suited Blizzard. He liked the sense of being away from people in the midst of the city.

As he opened the door, grimacing at the squeak and reminding himself to give the hinges a dot of oil, he felt like he was entering another world. Behind him were the twinkling street lights of the nearby city centre, the throb of rush hour car engines, the occasional peep of a horn and the distant rumble of a goods train heading for the chemical works on the river-bank. Inside, dimly illuminated by a stark single light bulb, which sputtered into life when he managed to find the switch on the wall, cursing as he barked his fingers, was a tangle of pieces of scrap metal and old, rusted tools, in the middle of which stood Blizzard's great love, an old railway engine.

Blizzard could trace his interest in steam trains back to his childhood in rural Lincolnshire when he used to watch the engines thunder along the line at the bottom of their garden. His passion had been fostered as a young boy through his grandfather, who had been a shed-master in Yorkshire during the war. As a child, Blizzard had devoured books about steam engines and, when he grew up, the fascination remained, a tingle still running down his spine whenever he heard the long whistle or saw the trails of billowing steam at railway carnivals.

Fifteen years ago, he had formed the Hafton Railway Appreciation Society, a small group of enthusiastic volunteers who used their spare time to rescue steam locomotives and lovingly restore them. Blizzard was noted for his encyclopaedic knowledge, even among the group of old railmen who knew so much themselves, and such was his expertise that he had edited their quarterly magazine for several years.

The current project was much more than a rusting old loco to Blizzard as he switched on the small heater, filled the kettle, struggled into grease-stained blue overalls and stood surveying the engine as he waited for the water to boil. The Silver Flyer had plied the line between the city and the Midlands for many years until taken out of commission in the 1960s during the death throes of the golden age of steam. For a long time no one seemed to know where she was, even though she had lain, sad and neglected in the railway shed behind the main station for all that time. Blizzard had stumbled across her while investigating a serious assault on the nearby wasteland, standing in amazement as he scraped off the rust to reveal the nameplate.

The society started raising the cash to buy and renovate her, driven by the dream that one day The Flyer—or as he knew her, The Old Lady—would steam again. Of course,

Blizzard had the mickey taken out of him by fellow officers, and more than one or two cocky villains, but he did not care. Whenever the demands of his job allowed him the spare time, he could be found up to his elbows in grease, a contented smile on his face as he brought the rusting parts back into use. Those villains who jested behind his back about his hobby would perhaps not have been as ready to make the joke had they known what else John Blizzard did in the engine shed. As he sat and worked, he thought, and as he thought, cases crystalized in his mind. In his experience, complex cases were foggy and confused in their early days but more than one successful line of inquiry had come from his loving work on the locomotive.

As David Colley hurled himself around the pitch on the other side of the city, tackling ferociously and grasping the rugby ball with gusto, John Blizzard worked quietly without interruption, popping out only for a bag of fish and chips. When he got back, another of the society members, a white-haired former train-driver was there, and they brewed up again and worked and yarned the night away with tales of steam locos, delighting in their rich memories. As they did, Colley showered, left the changing rooms and grabbed a quick pint with his teammates before heading back for a cosy night in with Jay.

It was just before midnight when John

Blizzard and his friend, realizing with a start that time had run away with them, chuckled and snapped out the light in the shed and walked across the wasteland to their cars, broken glass crunching beneath their feet. Watching his friend drive off, Blizzard gazed up at the stars twinkling in the clear sky. In the distance he could hear the rumbling of a train, the sound carrying for miles through the still night air. For some reason, a line from a Bruce Springsteen song popped into his head. What was it now? Something about a freight train running through the middle of his head? Something like that. It would come to him. He would play the tape as he drove home. Colley had lent it to him to, as he had put it, 'educate' his boss.

Around him, as he unlocked the car door, the city started to settle down apart from the few late bars which bothered to stay open on a Tuesday night. Even they were quiet and almost empty. It was, thought Blizzard, his favourite time of day. Not many people around, the streets pretty much deserted and peace settling on a city which boasted that it never slept but which grabbed forty winks when it thought no one was looking.

CHAPTER FOURTEEN

Colley hobbled into Blizzard's office shortly after eight next morning, wincing as he lowered himself tentatively into the chair. The chief inspector, sitting behind his desk, eyed his sergeant with amusement.

'I thought,' he said at length, 'that last night was supposed to be a practice?'

'You know what Denny Whatmore is like,' grimaced Colley, twisting in the seat so that his injured knee was not too painful.

'Say no more,' nodded Blizzard. 'They've never had a lot of brains in Traffic.'

'Anyway,' said Colley mischievously, 'how was your night with the Puffing Billy?'

Blizzard smiled, enjoying the joke. Officers at Abbey Road had learnt that, unless you wanted to earn yourselves one of those wilting glares from the chief inspector, you referred to The Flyer with respect. Only Colley seemed able to get away with it.

'It was fine, thank you.'

'Did you come to any conclusions while you were polishing the worple sprocket?' asked Colley, roaring with laughter and ducking as the chief inspector hurled his desk diary at him.

The book came to rest at the feet of Detective Inspector Graham Ross, the head of forensics who had just entered the room. He picked it up and replaced it on the desk. Usually, he appreciated their humour, joining in the banter, if always a touch respectfully towards the chief inspector—but not this time. Blizzard ran his eye up and down the officer's usual immaculate attire, a charcoal grey suit, red silk tie and crisp white shirt with the top button fastened.

'You're not modelling for Versace again are you?' he asked.

'I may be before the day is over,' said Ross glumly, sitting down and turning heavy eyes on Blizzard.

'What's up?' asked the chief inspector affably. 'Run out of freshly laundered handkerchiefs, perhaps?'

Colley smirked.

'I missed something,' said Ross, shifting uncomfortably in his seat, his boyish features troubled.

'What do you mean?' asked Blizzard sharply, the levity of a second before banished.

'I was so preoccupied with Josh Holdsworth that I didn't think enough about David Reed.'

'What about him?'

'I simply assumed that because he was lying on the floor with a serious head wound and a chunk of rock next to him that it must have been hurled through the window.'

'So did we all,' said Blizzard. 'If there was a mistake, we all made it.'

'I appreciate the comment,' replied Ross gratefully. 'We have been up against it the last couple of days, what with Josh Holdsworth and that armed robbery and the attack on the old dear . . .'

'Forget the excuses, Graham, just get to the point.'

'Sorry. When I reviewed the notes on David Reed something was a bit off. The angles didn't seem quite right so I went to the hostel last night to check it out again.' He leaned forward and looked at them earnestly. 'I reckoned it was highly unlikely that the rock came through that window.'

'What?' exclaimed Blizzard.

'So I went up to the hospital first thing this morning—wanted to make sure I was right before I came to fall on my sword.'

'How is he?' asked Colley.

'Still sedated—they are getting pretty worried about him. It's a bad skull fracture.'

'So what did you find out?' asked Blizzard.

'The staff nurse reckons he was hit twice— and there's no way a flying rock could do that.'

'Are you sure?'

'Yes. By good fortune, the nurse who cleaned him up in A and E had just been switched to the ward,' said Ross. 'She remembers having to pick out a small splinter of wood from the wound just after he was brought in.'

'Jesus,' gasped Colley.

'Keep him out of this,' said Blizzard drily. 'He's caused enough trouble as it is. So what was the weapon then? Nothing was found at the church.'

'Yeah, but we didn't exactly look hard, did we?' pointed out the sergeant.

'Exactly,' said Ross. 'So, I went back to the church and had another look. Hidden in the men's toilet cistern in the hostel was a wooden bookend from David Reed's office. It is at the lab at the moment but it has a dent in it. I am sure it was used to strike him and the rock was designed to throw us off the scent.'

And he looked at them glumly.

'It certainly worked.'

'Bloody hell,' exclaimed Blizzard, leaping to his feet and struggling into his suit jacket. 'That's got to mean that the person who killed Josh Holdsworth is the same person who attacked David Reed, don't you reckon, Sergeant?'

'Good chance,' agreed Colley, struggling to his feet and wincing in pain from his injured knee as he followed the chief inspector.

As they reached the door, Colley limping badly, Blizzard glanced back at the disconsolate Ross, who was still sitting in the chair, staring at the floor.

'Good work, Graham,' he said.

'I missed it,' protested Ross, only too aware of Blizzard's occasional rants when officers made mistakes which he thought had been avoidable.

'But you got it in the end,' said Blizzard, nodding reassuringly, 'and it hadn't even occurred to me and Hopalong Cassidy here.'

'And it's achieved more than all those worple sprockets put together,' added Colley.

'Worple sprockets?' asked a bemused Ross.

'Worple sprockets,' nodded Colley, tapping the side of his nose knowledgeably and wincing as he recalled he had been thumped there the night before.

The two detectives walked from the room, leaving a mightily relieved Graham Ross pondering on the vagaries of life, musing over what worple sprockets were and wondering if his legs would ever stop trembling.

CHAPTER FIFTEEN

Also trembling was Glenda Rutherford, the 49-year-old the assistant night manager at St Mary's Hostel. A shy and retiring woman with prim and proper features, mousy hair immaculately combed and tied up in a bob, yellow woollen cardigan and tartan skirt, the shoes cleaned and sensible, she sat staring fearfully at the two detectives as they sat in the office where David Reed had been attacked on the Sunday night.

The detectives had arrived at the hostel

suspicion onto the protestors for the attack on David Reed,' he interrupted curtly, 'when in fact, I think you and I need to talk about how your vicar is tied up with all this.'

The effect of his words on Rose-Harvey was remarkable and the detectives watched the young man in amazement. It was as if someone had slapped him. He seemed to start, taking a step backwards, the colour draining from his face. It took him a moment or two to regain his composure—and even then he remained visibly shaken.

'What on earth can you mean?' he blustered, but the voice betrayed his anxiety.

Blizzard smiled inwardly. He did not like people who took control of situations—that was his job—and he had definitely regained the initiative over the church leader now. There was clearly much more to the Reverend Henry Sanders than people were letting on. And Rose-Harvey knew it.

'So where is the vicar?' he asked, taking a couple of steps to stand within inches of Rose-Harvey and staring into his eyes.

Rose-Harvey turned his head slightly, refusing to meet the officer's steely gaze.

'I am afraid I do not know,' he said uncomfortably.

'Poppycock!'

'It's true,' he said evasively. 'You see, Henry has gone . . .'

'Gone?' exclaimed the chief inspector.

'Gone,' nodded Rose-Harvey, holding up the bank statement in his hand and adding bitterly as his composure deserted him completely, 'and he has taken the church's money with him!'

CHAPTER SIXTEEN

The remainder of Wednesday was taken up in a flurry of activity. The vicar had indeed taken church money with him, £28,000 of it, obtained by using forged signatures and bogus ledger entries over a period of months. Edgar Rose-Harvey was devastated. Such a crime went completely against his Christian faith but he seemed, in conversations with the detectives, more anxious about the effect the bad publicity would have on the church than the loss of the money. He even asked if it was possible to hush the incident up but the officers had stamped firmly on the idea.

The likelihood that David Reed had been deliberately attacked rather than the innocent victim of a stone-throwing incident threw a whole new complexion on the case and, in addition to researching the background of the sticky-fingered vicar, Blizzard ordered his team to begin checks on parishioners and to recheck the residents of the hostel. He was searching for a possible motive, a link between the attack on the hostel worker, the murder of Josh Holdsworth and the disappearance of the vicar, a chink in their stories, something, anything, to give his inquiry more focus. Checks into the reverend's background proved the most interesting and had, by the end of the day, hardened him as a prime suspect in the detectives' minds. It emerged that the vicar had only been a clergyman for twelve years: before that he had been a butcher, running his own business in southern England before closing it to pursue a career in the cloth. After two other postings, he had finally found his way to St Mary's, where he quickly proved himself a popular and wise vicar, whose services were innovative and inspiring and whose pastoral work was energetic and compassionate. Obtaining these facts proved easy, illiciting anything further, however, proved more difficult, most parishioners strangely reluctant to do anything but utter the kind of bland platitudes the detectives had heard all afternoon. Throughout those conversations, though, it became clear that the vicar disapproved of some of the methods of the evangelicals who had taken over the church.

It was towards late afternoon, however, that Colley tracked down a parishioner who was more forthcoming, a situation helped by the fact that both the sergeant and James Calvert, a 38-year-old fresh-faced businessman who ran a property letting agency, were keen rugby players and knew each other vaguely from matches. Colley had bumped into Calvert outside the church and had persuaded him to talk. Calvert, at first reluctant like all the others, eventually agreed on condition that it was away from the church. Indeed, throughout their conversation in the street outside St Mary's, his eyes darted this way and that, as if he were afraid that they were being watched. So, they went to his spartan office in a shabby row of converted terraced houses a mile from St Mary's Church. There, Calvert loosened his tie, threw his suit jacket over the back of his chair and opened the filing cabinet, lifting out a bottle of whisky and a couple of glasses.

'Snifter?' he asked.

'Better not,' said Colley. 'Duty and all that.'

Calvert poured himself a large one and sat down behind his desk.

'So what do you want to know?' he asked keenly. 'Everything,' replied Colley. 'There is something not right with that church.'

'Tell me about it,' nodded Calvert, taking a large gulp of whisky, and leaning forward. 'Listen, I don't want dragging into this, right? I don't want anyone to know I have spoken to you.'

'Why?'

'Like you said, there's something not right,' replied Calvert enigmatically. 'St Mary's was a nice church once. I started going when I was a kid. I was a Scout—only because it got me in with the Guides, mind.'

Colley smiled.

'It was always a happy place. Full of Christian spirit. Then they came along.'

'The evangelicals?'

'Yeah.' Calvert took another gulp of whisky, draining the glass and filling it up again. 'Don't get me wrong. I don't mind born-again Christians, those boring stuffy old services had to change, but this lot are creepy. It's more than tambourines.'

'Creepy?'

'Yeah,' and he shuddered. 'Like they're always watching you in case you do something wrong. And anyone who disagrees with them gets frozen out. I keep my head down.'

'And what about the vicar?'

'It was weird. He seemed spooked by them. That Edgar Rose-Harvey character, he's a nasty piece of work. It was like Henry Sanders had no power at all after they arrived. They made all the decisions. He looked scared when Rose-Harvey or one of his pals walked into the room. The atmosphere was awful. And he hated the hostel.'

'But I thought that was the church's big project?'

'It was *their* project, not Henry's. He hated the idea of paedophiles and the like staying just yards from the church. Even complained to social services.'

'So why didn't he leave if he was so against it?'

'Not that easy in the church,' said Calvert, taking another gulp. 'Got to jump through lots of hoops if you want a posting—and Rose-Harvey and his bunch were holding them.'

'We think the vicar has stolen money from the church,' said Colley.

Calvert whistled in surprise.

'Never had him down for that sort of thing, I have to say.'

'And he was the last person to see David Reed before he was injured.'

'Jesus,' breathed Calvert.

'No, we've got a witness to say he was elsewhere,' replied Colley drily.

There was a moment's silence then Calvert burst into laughter.

'Sorry, bad taste,' said Colley. 'Did you know Josh Holdsworth?'

'Saw him a few times, came to the church with his mum. He was one of the Scouts and I think the vicar was friendly with the family. Often used to see him talking to the kid's mother, Marian I think she's called. There were rumours . . . ?'

'Rumours?'

'That they were very friendly,'—Calvert took another slug—'if you get my drift.'

'And were they?'

'Dunno. Mind, once when I was driving past the end of their street, I saw him coming out of their house.'

'What about Steve Holdsworth?'

'Bad bit of work,' said Calvert firmly. 'Never knew him and don't want to neither. There was talk that he hit the kid. I saw Josh with a black eye one day.'

'Did he know about the affair?'

'Do you think the vicar would still have been walking if he did?'

'OK, thanks,' said Colley, standing up. 'You've been very helpful.'

'Just remember what I said,' and Calvert pointed a finger at him. 'Keep my name out of this.'

'I will,' said Colley, pausing at the door and gesturing to the whisky bottle on the table. 'Oh, and I wouldn't drive home if I were you.'

'Can't,' said Calvert with a smile. 'Got banned two months ago.'

There's a surprise,' murmured Colley, and walked out into the gathering gloom of late afternoon to find Blizzard parked outside.

'Come on,' he said, winding down the window. 'I've got a little surprise for Mr Holdsworth.'

'Ooh, goody, I like surprises!' said Colley and clambered in.

Twenty minutes later they were back in the living room of the Holdsworths' neat little house, Steve defiant and obstructive as ever, Marian as cowed as she was last time. She had clearly been crying. A lot.

'Mr Holdsworth,' said Blizzard, 'we have been doing some checking up on you.'

'Oh, yeah?'

'Yes,' nodded Blizzard, ignoring the big man's suspicious glares. 'Turns out that Northern CID questioned you four years ago for hitting your son outside a pub following a football match.'

'He were being lippy!'

'Indeed,' said Blizzard, glancing down at a crumpled piece of paper which he had fished out of his suit jacket pocket. 'And three years ago, Josh was taken to hospital with a broken arm and social services came to interview you—as did one of our officers.'

'Nowt were ever proved,' exclaimed Holdsworth angrily.

'Indeed, but it is interesting given that your son has just been killed, is it not?'

Marian Holdsworth burst into tears and Steve Holdsworth turned baleful eyes on the chief inspector and seemed about to lunge at him when something stopped him. Mastering his fury, he sat back in his chair.

'I ain't got nothing to do with my son's death,' he said defiantly. 'I were on a rig in the North Sea.'

'But were you?' replied Blizzard. 'Does the name Edgy Brattan mean anything to you, Mr Holdsworth?'

It was as if the big man had been punched. He gaped at the detective for a moment or two, mouth opening and shutting several times, then slumped back into his chair, looking for all the world like a deflated balloon.

'Who is this Edgy Brattan?' asked his wife, surveying her stunned husband with amazement.

He was a powerful man used to being in control yet here he was poleaxed by the mention of a single name.

'He's your supervisor on the rig, isn't he, Steve?'

The big man nodded feebly.

'They go way back, Mrs Holdsworth, they're good friends, will do anything for each other. Actually, it was Edgy Brattan who offered to fly your husband home when we contacted the rig to tell him that Josh had been killed. A truly generous gesture. Except, you were not on the rig, were you, Steve?'

Holdsworth shook his head. The transformation had been remarkable: his face was ashen, his cheeks were sunken and his eyes darted round the room like those of a caged animal.

'In fact,' continued Blizzard, 'Edgy Brattan made it all up because your husband had flown over to the mainland on the Friday helicopter.'

'What?' gasped Marian, turning horrified eyes on her husband, who desperately tried to advert his gaze.

'And unless he comes up with a good

explanation, I have to think the worst about that,' said Blizzard, fixing the oilman with a piercing gaze. 'Steve, anything to say?'

Holdsworth shook his head.

'In which case,' said Blizzard, gesturing to Colley, 'I have no alternative but to arrest you on suspicion of the murder of Josh Holdsworth. Tell him his rights, please, Sergeant.'

And, as Marian Holdsworth slumped in her chair in floods of tears, the detectives led the stunned Steve Holdsworth into the cold night air.

CHAPTER SEVENTEEN

'Did you never fancy having kids, John?'

The question came from Jay Priest, the slim, willowy redhead with whom David Colley lived, who had settled down on her sofa with a glass of wine in her hand.

Colley had invited Blizzard back to their home, a terraced house a mile or so from the police station, after another late finish at work. Acutely aware that they had a decent but circumstantial case against Steve Holdsworth, the detectives had held a hurried discussion with Arthur Ronald, who had his coat on and was heading for the door when they arrived at his office. They had agreed that the detectives needed to strike rapidly to take advantage of Holdsworth's confusion, a plan which seemed a good one in Ronald's office but did not work out that way in the airless interview-room.

Holdsworth had called a solicitor and after refusing to answer several questions, had claimed that he felt ill. The doctor was called and diagnosed a racing heartbeat, recommending that questioning be suspended and that Holdsworth be taken back to the cell and allowed to rest. Blizzard, convinced it was all a con, had argued vociferously with the medical man but had been comprehensively defeated when the doctor has asked him if he wished to explain to the chief constable, should any harm come to the prisoner, why he ignored expert advice. Blizzard had thrown up his hands and stalked off down the corridor, muttering something about 'bloody experts' and leaving Colley to smooth the doctor's ruffled feathers. It wasn't the first time he had been called upon to do such a job and he achieved it with his usual diplomatic charm.

By the time all that had been sorted out, it was approaching nine o'clock so Colley, uncomfortably aware that his dinner had long since burnt itself to a crisp in the oven, had suggested a take-away round at his house. Jay had given them a frosty reception at first, but when Blizzard gave that rueful smile of his, proffered an affectionate peck on the check and held up a bottle of her favourite white wine she had relented and let them in. An hour later, the take-away had been consumed, Blizzard grimacing as he always did when eating delivered pizzas. It was a little known fact about the chief inspector that he was a talented cook of Italian food and although he ate take-aways when needs must, he usually objected strongly on principle to the creations which turned up on the doorstep. Having made his obligatory negative remarks, however, to knowing smiles from Colley and his girlfriend, he had devoured his meal and now all three were sitting in the tastefully decorated room with its pastel shades and rustic prints, the soft light afforded by a couple of table lamps and the flickering fake coal fire. Blizzard was in an armchair, glass of wine in his hand—he liked to switch between wine and beer—Colley was in another, sticking with a can of bitter, and Jay was curled up on the sofa. It had always been an easy relationship, helped, they all thought, by their golden rule on social occasions—no shop. However, Jay's question was perilously close to breaking that rule and Blizzard considered carefully for a moment before replying.

'I think we did,' he said at length, recalling the years with his wife.

'Think?' repeated Jay.

'My wife wanted them, not sure I did,' explained Blizzard. 'Not fair when you do a job like ours.'

Noticing her expression and remembering the tensions between Jay and David over the issue, he rapidly realized his gaffe and said hurriedly, 'Not that I mean . . . what I . . . look, all I am saying . . . I didn't mean that you and—'

Jay chuckled. 'Not sure I have ever seen you ruffled, Mr Blizzard,' she said.

He smiled that rueful smile again and glanced at Colley, whose own expression, briefly disturbed at his friend's thoughtless comment, now reassured him.

'Sorry, it's just that I never had much affinity with kids, although,'—Blizzard leaned forward conspiratorially—'as long as you don't tell anyone else, I'd hate it to get round the station, but it is true that I was one once.'

Colley roared with laughter.

'I very much doubt that,' he said. 'I reckon you were born forty-something.'

'Maybe. Anyway, why do you ask about kids, Jay?'

'This case of yours,' and she held up her hand. 'OK, I know, I know, no shop.'

'It's all right,' said Blizzard.

'David doesn't ever talk about his work,' said Jay, reaching out a hand to her partner.

It was readily taken.

'It's not fair,' nodded Blizzard. 'No point depressing everyone else. But sometimes it helps to talk to someone else about it. And I sure as hell can't make head nor tail of this one.'

'But to kill a child,' said Jay in disbelief, shaking her head. 'Particularly your own, I mean, who could ever do that, John?'

'Some people do,' replied Blizzard, and he stared into the flickering fire.

It was some moments before anyone spoke then Colley asked, 'So are you sure Steve Holdsworth did it?'

Blizzard, lifted from his reverie, sighed and took another sip of wine.

'I don't know, David, I really do not know.'

Then, his mood suddenly lightening, he reached for the wine bottle, topped up Jay's glass then his own and beamed.

'This is nice,' he said.

'The wine?' asked Jay.

'No, the company. It's nice to spend time talking to someone attractive and intelligent—and David puts the odd word in as well.'

The cushion hurled by the sergeant flew by his head as his boss ducked. Blizzard's beam was dispelled, however, when he heard the muffled bark of Bruce, the couple's German Shepherd.

Bruce was a former police dog, drummed out of the force for poor behaviour and the couple loved him. Blizzard detested dogs, a legacy he always said, of having a paper round when he was a teenager. He still claimed to have the scar where a dog bit him while he was delivering papers but no one had ever seen it—or dared ask where it was. So, whenever he came round to their house, Blizzard always insisted that the dog be locked away. He listened then gave a broad smile.

'On the other hand, that's my kind of dog—locked in the shed!'

And suddenly, for a few moments at least, it seemed as if the cares of the day had left him.

CHAPTER EIGHTEEN

But they were back the next morning. And in force. Blizzard usually liked the last Thursday of the month—pay day—but this one had started badly and was getting worse. The first problem was the weakness of his case against Steve Holdsworth, the second one was the chief constable badgering Arthur Ronald who was, reluctantly, badgering Blizzard for news, the third one was the missing vicar and the fourth was Albert Macklin, neither of whom had been sighted. The night before, the chief constable had, apparently, been at a community forum in the area which included St Mary's and had been assailed by a fired-up Margaret Hatton and some of her supporters, who demanded to know why Albert Macklin had been allowed to escape the clutches of the police when he was the prime suspect in the murder of Josh Holdsworth. The chief's discomfiture was increased when a television crew arrived and it became clear that Margaret Hatton had set the whole thing up, hijacking what he had supposed to be a routine meeting for which the date was settled weeks before.

An uncomfortable chief constable had endured twenty minutes, acutely aware that the cameras were filming close-ups of his perspiring forehead, then stalked out, refusing to answer any more questions. Footage of his humiliating retreat, which had been accompanied by the protestors' boos and jeers, had made it on to the national television news that morning and the tabloids, whose interest had been waning slightly, had found it suddenly reignited. As a result, the press office had been bombarded with calls from national media reporters demanding the chief's response and the face of Albert Macklin was featured on television screens throughout the land. The situation was not helped by Margaret Hatton's somewhat rash demand that the chief constable consider resigning over the matter.

All this had been conveyed to Blizzard by a world-weary Arthur Ronald just before the chief inspector and his sergeant went into interview Steve Holdsworth at 9.30, an interview which did not go well. Three hours later, the detectives, Blizzard in rolled-up shirt sleeves, Colley retaining his suit jacket, were getting nowhere in their questioning of the prisoner, who was still dressed in his grubby T-shirt and tatty jeans.

'So,' said Blizzard, leaning forward over the table and glaring at Steve Holdsworth, whose eyes flashed defiance. 'You deny causing any of the injuries to your son in the past and you deny being anywhere near the city at the weekend but you will not tell me where you were.'

'I ain't saying nothing,' growled Holdsworth, unbowed by the chief inspector's annoyance and glancing at his lawyer for reassurance.

'But it does not look good for you if you keep quiet; can't you see that?'

'On the contrary, Chief Inspector,' said Holdsworth's lawyer, a weasel-faced man in his thirties, with sallow cheeks and thin lips and sharply dressed in a black suit. 'You have nothing on my client.'

Blizzard sighed. His views on lawyers were very clear. He regarded them the same way as he regarded the slugs which kept eating the lettuce he tried to grow in his garden: he knew they existed but he could not quite see the point of them. To combat the slugs he threw down pellets. To date, he had been unable to find a similarly suitable antidote to lawyers.

'Listen,' said the chief inspector angrily, 'this is not a game, I am investigating the murder of this man's son. I think he had something to do with it and unless he tells me where he was when he was supposed to be on the oil rig, I have no alternative to keep thinking it, do I?'

'I have advised my client to say nothing,' said the lawyer smoothly.

'Pha!!' exclaimed Blizzard, standing up quickly, sending his chair crashing backwards, and stalking furiously from the room, leaving Colley to pick it up.

'Is my client free to go?' asked the lawyer.

'What do you think?' replied the sergeant curtly, following his chief inspector from the interview-room.

Outside in the corridor, he found Blizzard leaning against the wall, a dark expression on his face. He knew that expression, it was the one which the chief inspector's face assumed when he was not in control of a situation, when he knew they were not in possession of all the facts and that people were holding things back. Blizzard hated that, as did Colley.

'Sorry,' mumbled the chief inspector.

'No need to apologize.'

'I shouldn't have lost it—but we are struggling big time,' sighed the chief inspector, turning heavy eyes on the sergeant. 'If he keeps this up we will have no option but to let him go.'

'Maybe he didn't do it,' ventured Colley, not sure if the comment would elicit an explosion of anger from his boss.

It didn't.

'Yeah, maybe,' admitted the chief inspector.

'The tests do suggest he was not the one who sexually assaulted his son. But if so, why lie about where he was the afternoon the kid was killed. And why—?'

But he got no further because his mobile phone rang. He listened for a moment then said with a glint in his eye.

'You know, I have been to church more times in the past six days that in my entire previous life—Glenda Rutherford wishes to see us!'

Twenty minutes later they were back in the office at the hostel with a still clearly distressed Glenda Rutherford sitting opposite them, next to a scowling Edgar Rose-Harvey.

'You have something to tell us, I think,' said Blizzard.

She nodded, struggling for the composure needed to tell her story.

'I have not been straight with you, Chief Inspector,' she said at length.

'You'd be the first if you had,' grunted Blizzard.

Rose-Harvey glared at him.

'I didn't want to say anything because it looks bad for the vicar,' Glenda said, dabbing her tear-filled eyes with a tissue. 'You see, that night David Reed was attacked he had just told me something . . .'

There was a pause.

'Something?' asked Blizzard.

'Yes.' She took a deep breath. 'One of

David's jobs was to do the accounts for the church, including the hostel. He told me that he had discovered that twenty-eight thousand pounds was missing.'

'How did he find out?'

'The bank had queried something on the Friday; they were not happy about the signature on a document. David had been checking over the weekend and discovered that someone had been taking money and trying to cover their tracks.'

'And had he told anyone about this?'

'Yes,' and her voice dropped to an almost inaudible whisper. 'Henry Sanders. He believed the vicar was taking the money.'

'And why, pray, didn't he tell me?' demanded Rose-Harvey, who had been listening with increasing anger. 'It's my bloody church!'

'And there was me thinking it belonged to the risen Lord,' murmured Blizzard.

Rose-Harvey glared at him again then turned his attention back to the trembling Glenda Rutherford.

'Well?' he demanded.

'He wanted to be sure,' she said.

'Is that why the vicar went to see him here that night?' asked Colley.

'Yes,' she nodded. 'David said he needed to discuss it with him.'

'And now David Reed is lying seriously ill in a hospital bed and the vicar has disappeared,' said Blizzard pointedly.

'With our money,' added Rose-Harvey angrily. 'I just cannot believe that he would do this. And after we gave him another chance—'

'Chance?' asked Blizzard sharply. 'What do you mean *chance*?'

'I suppose you had to find out sometime,' sighed Rose-Harvey. 'The vicar is a sinner.'

'Frankly, the lot of you seem to have broken most of the Ten Commandments,' grunted Blizzard.

'Indeed,' replied Rose-Harvey with a wan smile. 'But Henry sinned more than most, Chief Inspector. In fact, he was quite good at it.'

'Go on.'

'After we took over the church, we became suspicious about him, so we did some checking with his previous church. It just so happened I knew my counterpart a little bit; we had met a couple of times at evangelical conventions. Anyway, he said the vicar had been asked to leave because money had gone missing and they thought he was taking it.'

'Did they call the police?'

'Certainly not,' said Rose-Harvey in animated fashion. 'Henry had denied it. Besides, there's precious few people coming to church without frightening them off with the thought that their collection money is going to pay for the vicar's little peccadilloes.'

'Is that what he was doing?'

'Apparently so.'

'The peccadillo being Marian Holdsworth?'

'I believe so,' and he added hurriedly. 'But there was no evidence he was doing it here. The books seemed to be in order.'

'And was there any suggestion that he might have been acting inappropriately with children?' asked the chief inspector.

'There had been some suggestions,' admitted Rose-Harvey guardedly.

'And you let him stay in his job?' exclaimed Blizzard.

'Yes we did,' said Rose-Harvey, adding quickly when he saw their horrified expressions, 'Henry assured us it was all malicious gossip. I believed him, Chief Inspector. We had seen nothing to suggest he was up to anything here.'

'But surely, even if you had suspicions, you should have let him go—why keep him on?' said Colley curiously, as Blizzard walked over to the window and stared out at the overcast sky, shaking his head in disbelief at what he was hearing.

'Ah, Sergeant, Sergeant,' replied Rose-Harvey sadly. 'You and I can never ever be the same. You see, our belief in the power of Christ is total. Why help the good people when the Lord sees ten times more reward in one sinner who repents? Did not Christ say when He was on the cross—?'

'Spare me the bloody sermon,' growled

Blizzard, 'and answer the question!'

'I am answering your question,' said Rose-Harvey archly. 'Our group had just arrived at the church and we were looking for ways to make a real difference. We wanted to give Henry another chance for the good to triumph over the evil in his soul. It was an ideal opportunity to test the power of our faith. The Church is too staid, Chief Inspector, it needs to confront the big issues. That is why we set up the hostel and why we kept on a vicar who had sinned.'

'Did the congregation know about his past?' asked Blizzard.

'Oh, no.' Rose-Harvey shook his head furiously. 'But it was enough that we could see the power of the Lord working within him.'

'And working miracles on his bank balance, too,' retorted Blizzard sourly.

'Yes, but in life,' said Rose-Harvey, his voice slipping into preaching mode, 'you have to take risks for what you believe. You have to reach out and touch—'

'Oh, for God's sake!' exclaimed Blizzard.

'There,' beamed Rose-Harvey, 'You're getting the idea!'

CHAPTER NINETEEN

'So,' asked Max Randall, unable to hide the disappointment in his voice, 'are we saying this is all about some unfrocked vicar?'

It was early evening and he was sitting with Arthur Ronald, John Blizzard, David Colley and Alex Mather in a seedy roadside café on the main motorway out of the city, just over the border into the neighbouring force area so that local officers would not accidentally spot them. The team, who had just polished off eggs and bacon and were sipping their second mugs of tea, had become used to such tactics over the years during which they had investigated the sex ring. The venue had been Randall's idea a year or so before and even Arthur Ronald, who had bridled at the sergeant's claim that a senior police officer was involved, never demurred from such cloak-and-dagger stuff. He had not raised a murmur of objection either when Randall had suggested the café for this evening's gathering. Although the superintendent constantly rebuked himself for doubting colleagues, he could not get rid of the nagging feeling that the grizzled veteran was right and that the Keeper team was being watched.

The café might not have been particularly pleasant but it was one of the places the

Operation Keeper team met when they needed to talk away from prying eyes. It was a single-storey building with cracked yellow lino, formica tables covered with encrusted ketchup and tea stains and walls decorated in drab brown wallpaper, peeling at the edges due to damp. It was a typical Thursday night and the clientele were the usual burly truckers, some of whom eyed the group suspiciously, fearing they may be Department of Transport inspectors, and reminding themselves to check their tacographs when they got back to their cabs. But after a few minutes, when it became clear that the men in the corner were not interested in anything but their intense conversation, the drivers relaxed and returned to their meals.

'Maybe,' said Blizzard guardedly, cradling his mug of lukewarm tea, one eye on a couple of dodgy-looking truckers who had just walked in; that was the cost of being a copper, he reflected, as the men ordered their meal and sat down at a table: you viewed everyone as a villain.

'Not that simple, surely?' said Mather, absent-mindedly picking at the remains of his meal with a fork. 'I can see an argument which says the vicar attacked David Reed because he was about to blow the whistle on him, but Josh Holdsworth? There is no link.'

'Ah, but what about the vicar's dodgy past?' asked Ronald, dubiously eying the scum forming on the top of his tea. 'Are you sure this is safe to drink?'

'I've had worse,' said Randall, peering into the superintendent's mug.

'Besides,' piped up Colley, sitting at the end of the table, 'it will come in handy for removing rust on your car—not that you high-ups have rusty cars, of course.'

Ronald gave him a sour look.

'I do,' said Blizzard glumly.

'Yes, I have been meaning to talk to you about . . .' began Ronald, but the chief inspector good-naturedly waved his protest away.

'Go on, David,' sighed Ronald. 'Are we sure we fancy this vicar?'

'The story about him does check out,' said Colley, stretching out his long legs and wincing as a stab of pain reminded him of his rugby injury. 'I talked to the bloke at his old church—another bloody happy-clappy type—and they did get rid of him for allegedly nicking cash.'

'So how come St Mary's took him on? He arrived before Rose-Harvey and all that, remember,' said Ronald.

'The church lied on his reference,' explained Colley.

'There's another of the commandments shattered,' grunted Blizzard. 'Not many left now.'

'And what about this suggestion that he was

doing things with kids?' asked Mather, clean-shaven and dressed tonight in a suit, having spent the day interviewing suspects, his undercover inquiry having come to a successful conclusion.

'The guy said it was only gossip. Nothing substantiated.'

'What did the local nick say?' asked Blizzard.

'Nothing reported,' replied Colley. 'No investigation, end of story as far as they were concerned.'

'That sounds familiar,' growled Randall, swilling his tea round in the mug. 'Every time we seem to be getting somewhere, we run into dead ends.'

'The fact remains,' said Mather, 'That it could be two different attackers, one who did David Reed, the other who killed the boy. Remember, Henry Sanders had no reason to kill Josh Holdsworth. The only motive could be if the kid knew about the vicar's cash fiddles.'

'Ah, but maybe he did,' said Colley, leaning forward. 'James Calvert reckons he and Marian Holdsworth were having an affair— what if the vicar was nicking the cash to run away with her?'

'Yes, but why kill him?' asked Blizzard dubiously.

'Maybe the kid changes his mind about it all,' mused Colley. 'Maybe he threatens to tell

Stevie boy and the vicar knows he's dead meat if that happens.'

'Or maybe he was worried that he would lose his job if it got out,' ventured Randall.

'Perhaps David is right,' said Mather. 'After all, what would happen if word got out that Sanders was stealing from the church?'

'He'd be sacked,' said Ronald.

'Worse, he'd be charged with theft, he couldn't expect to have it hushed up twice and he would probably go to prison. How long do you think a defrocked vicar would last in jail?'

'It's the most plausible option,' admitted Blizzard. 'And both of them were attacked with items from the church.'

'The other option is someone with a vendetta against the church. Like our friend Bob Maddox, for instance,' ventured Colley.

'I can't see him killing his best mate's boy,' said Randall dubiously.

'Trouble is,' said Blizzard, 'without more evidence I don't dare starting roping parishioners in willy nilly for questioning. We have already pushed it with our Mr Rose-Harvey—it can't be long before he puts in an official complaint.'

'Too provocative without evidence,' agreed Ronald. 'If we go on a fishing trip and we're wrong the press will have a field day.'

'So is Albert Macklin innocent?' asked Randall.

'It's beginning to look that way,' asserted

Ronald, adding as he noticed Blizzard's expression, 'You needn't look at me like that, John. You have got it into your mind that once guilty, always guilty. What if he isn't? What if you did scare him off and he's just done a runner?'

'I hear what you're saying,' said Blizzard. 'But me and Dave were discussing this earlier . . .'

He did not have time to finish his sentence because his mobile phone rang. He listened for a moment then announced,

'That was Tulley. I am afraid myself and the good sergeant are going to have to miss out on the delightful range of desserts,'—he glanced at the mouldering fruit scones on the counter—'Marian Holdsworth wishes to see us . . .'

CHAPTER TWENTY

'I have not been entirely honest with you, Chief Inspector,' said Marian Holdsworth, as they sat once more in her living-room, surrounded by her Christian icons.

'Now, where have I heard those words before?' murmured Blizzard, glancing at his sergeant. 'It seems that there is a special Eleventh Commandment for everyone linked to St Mary's—"Thou shalt lie through thine bloody back teeth"!'

'There is something I should have told you earlier,' she admitted.

'About you and the vicar?' asked Colley.

She started and gazed at him in amazement. 'How did you know?'

'It is our job to know,' replied Colley. 'How close were you, Mrs Holdsworth?'

'Before I answer that, are you going to release Steve?'

'I have no option,' shrugged Blizzard. 'There is nothing to link him to the death of your son. I don't know where he was over the weekend but there is nothing to suggest that he was down the canal.'

She nodded then sighed.

'He will kill me.'

'An unfortunate turn of phrase,' said Blizzard drily. 'Please tell us what you called us here for.'

'I can tell you where he was.'

'Go on,' and the chief inspector leaned forward in his chair.

'I didn't really believe it until you told me he wasn't on the rig. He has been having an affair for the past year. She lives in Barnsley. I suspected it for a while but six weeks ago, when he had his last shore leave, he told me he had to work instead. That weekend, Joshua fell ill with scarlet fever and I rang the rig to tell Steve. Whoever I talked to was not in on the secret and said Steve was not there, said he

148

had gone to see his girlfriend.'

'Does he know you know?' asked Colley.

She smiled weakly. 'No. And as you have now realized, I have a secret of my own, Sergeant. Over the last few months, myself and Henry Sanders had grown close, very close. In fact, Henry had asked me to leave Steve and go away with him.'

'And you said?' asked Blizzard.

'I said I would think about it.' Her eyes assumed a far-off expression. 'Henry is everything Steve is not, sensitive, gentle, caring—'

'And a thief,' interrupted Blizzard curtly.

'What do you mean?' she asked, the surprise appearing to be genuine.

'He stole money from the church.'

'Not Henry!' she exclaimed.

'That's what Edgar Rose-Harvey reckons.'

'That man!'

The words were almost spat out.

'Meaning?'

'Henry detested him, said it was difficult to see the Christian spirit in him.'

'To be honest,' sighed Blizzard, 'I am struggling to see the Christian spirit in any of you, Mrs Holdsworth. Did Josh know about Henry's offer to whisk you away into the sunset?'

'Yes,' nodded Marian, tears welling up as she thought of her lost son. 'Yes, he did.'

'And what did he think of it?'

'He liked Henry,' she sobbed. 'He didn't hurt him like . . .'

Her voice tailed off in mid-sentence. The detectives watched, sensing her turmoil. She stared at the ground for a moment, seemingly fascinated by the whirls in the carpet, then looked Blizzard straight in the eye.

'You will get nothing more from me,' she said firmly. 'I have said enough already. I wanted to talk to you because I guessed you would hear about me and Henry from someone at the church. People can be such gossips.'

'But we need to ask you about—'

'No more questions,' she said firmly.

And with that she stood up and left the room. Blizzard glanced round at a smiling Virgin Mary perched on the television set.

'What are you laughing at?' he growled, and the detectives let themselves out of the house.

'Like Max Randall said,' commented Colley once the detectives were back in the street, 'dead ends, always dead ends . . .'

Blizzard's mobile phone rang. He stood, leaning against the car, listening grimly, then stared across at his sergeant.

'It's time to go to church again,' he said bleakly.

'You're becoming quite religious in your old age,' quipped Colley.

'Well we are going to need some divine help from somewhere,' replied Blizzard, his voice

150

hard. 'Because this dead end is as dead as they come. Someone has just killed Glenda Rutherford!

CHAPTER TWENTY-ONE

Within three minutes, having passed through the cordon of flashing blue lights outside St Mary's, the detectives had joined two green-suited paramedics in the dimly lit church, gazing silently upon the twisted and crumpled body of Glenda Rutherford who lay on her front behind a row of chairs. She had clearly been struck from behind, possibly while kneeling in prayer, and it was not difficult to see the injury which killed her, a huge blood-caked gash in her head clear testament to a terrific blow. Her usually immaculate hair was dishevelled and bloodstained and her face was rivered with blood which had trickled down onto the same yellow cardigan she had been wearing when they interviewed her.

'Was she alive when you arrived?' Blizzard asked one of the paramedics.

'Just,' nodded the man. 'Died a few moments after we got to her. Nothing we could have done.'

'Did she say anything?'

'Fraid not.'

'OK, thanks for your help,' said Blizzard,

and the detectives watched in grim silence as the paramedics left the church.

For a few moments Blizzard said nothing, seemingly mesmerized by the corpse, so Colley walked round the church, eventually pushing open the unlocked door to the vestry, clicking on the light and gazing at the sight that met his eyes. There, neatly placed on a folded cassock on the table, was a bloodstained wooden bookstand.

'Better come in here,' he said, popping his head round the door.

Blizzard entered and looked at the bookstand.

'It wasn't difficult to find,' said Colley, walking back into the church to check that the stand was missing at the lectern from which the preachers gave their addresses. It was.

'Almost like it was planted,' breathed Blizzard, rejoining him in the church.

'Got to be the weapon.'

Colley knelt down and looked closer at Glenda Rutherford's blood-rivered face.

'There's no fear,' he said. 'She probably didn't know what was happening.'

'That makes two of us,' grunted Blizzard, noticing the shocked duty manager standing at the door to the church and walking briskly towards him.

The man's face was pale, the eyes haunted being the spectacles, the lips trembling. He was leaning against the door frame, hardly able to support himself.

'Did you find her?' asked Blizzard.

The young man nodded.

'What happened?'

'I was about to finish for the day,' said the man, after pausing to gather his composure, his voice quiet and tremulous. 'Glenda always went to pray before she started work. I heard her scream and ran in and . . .' His voice tailed off and he stared at the ceiling, trying to compose himself.

'Did you see anyone else?' asked the chief inspector.

'No. No one.'

Blizzard was about to ask another question when a movement caught his attention through one of the side windows. At first he was not sure quite what he was seeing but the closer he looked he realized that it was the shadow of a person outside, silhouetted against the street lights, moving stealthily along the edge of the church outside.

'Bloody hell!' yelled Blizzard, pointing to the window. 'David!'

The sergeant followed his gaze and sprang into action. With a few athletic bounds, knee injury forgotten, he was out of the church and hurtling through the front door, barging past the startled uniformed officer guarding it. Yelling for the constable to follow him, the sergeant careered round the side of the church to see a shape fleeing into the shadows of the garden. Colley, adrenaline driving away the pain in his knee, sprinted across the garden, cursing as he bounced off one of the trees, eyes focused on the fleeing man. At the end of the garden was a high wall beyond which were the backyards of terraced houses. For a second the man hesitated then spotted the compost bin, flipped himself onto it and with a superhuman effort, scrambled onto the top of the wall, nimbly avoiding the shards of cemented-in glass designed to deter burglars, and jumped down the other side. They heard a dustbin go flying and another pained yell from the man as he twisted his ankle on landing. Then there was a thunderous hammering on the back door of the house and a frantic shouting.

Colley also leapt onto the compost bin and hurled himself on top of the wall, crying out in pain as the glass sliced through his hand. Trying to ignore the agony, he glanced down into the yard and saw the man pounding on the door, then saw the kitchen light go on and the back door swing open. Confronted by a startled elderly man, the intruder barged into the house, knocking the pensioner over. The sergeant heard the old man's head smash against the wall. Colley gritted his teeth against the pain and leapt into the yard, crying out as he landed on his injured knee. The uniformed officer was beside him in a flash, hitting the ground hard, rolling over twice then helping the sergeant to his feet; together they rushed into the house, pausing for a moment to check the householder was all right.

The man lay motionless and the constable stayed behind to tend to him while the sergeant limped as fast as he could down the hallway, noticing in despair that the front door had been flung open and that the intruder had fled into the street. With a desperate lunge he threw himself out into the road and glanced desperately up and down but saw just parked cars and one or two people coming out of their houses to see what had caused the commotion. There was no sign of his quarry.

'Damn!' exclaimed Colley, forgetting his gashed hand, thumping the wall and wincing as the pain shot right up his arm. 'Damn, damn, damn!'

Within moments flashing blue lights converged on the street from both ends and uniformed officers poured from vehicles and fanned out to begin searching. A few moments later, Blizzard appeared, blowing slightly and eyeing the scene grimly. He approached his sergeant, who was now sitting on a low front wall wrapping a handkerchief round his hand, having realized that it was bleeding profusely.

'Are you OK?' asked Blizzard.

'Yes,' nodded Colley, teeth still gritted with the pain.

'Doesn't look like it.'

'I'm OK.'

'We'll get the ambulance guys to take a look at you. Did you get a good look at him?'

'A bit,' nodded Colley. 'When the guy put his kitchen light on and opened his back door. Five ten, five eleven, slim, dark hair, green anorak, dark trousers. Didn't see his face.'

'Young, old?'

'Not sure.'

'Doesn't sound like Bob Maddox.'

'No way.'

'Could it have been the vicar?' asked the chief inspector.

'He was the right build,' nodded Colley.

'Not sure a vicar would have run like that, though,' replied the chief inspector sitting next to Colley and placing a reassuring arm on his shoulder while eying the deep gash and the sergeant's pale face anxiously.

'Don't be so sure,' said Colley, wrapping the crimson handkerchief tighter round the gaping wound. 'According to one of the parishioners, he never drank, ate the right things, went jogging most days—and was a champion sprinter when he was younger.'

'Bloody marvellous,' sighed Blizzard then turned as a uniformed inspector approached.

'Anything, Bob?'

' 'Fraid not. Looks like he's got away, we've got people searching the surrounding streets.'

'What about the bloke he knocked over in the house?' ask Colley.

The inspector nodded to an ambulance

edging its way along the street, watched by a growing band of interested onlookers.

'Chap in his early sixties, nasty bang to his head. They're taking him to hospital but it doesn't seem that bad. You need to get that hand seen to.'

Colley nodded, suddenly feeling faint as the world started to spin, and allowed the inspector to help him to the ambulance. Blizzard sat deep in thought for a moment or two then watched grimly as the householder was brought out on a stretcher.

'This,' he said to himself, 'has not been a good day.'

CHAPTER TWENTY-TWO

Friday didn't start much better as Margaret Hatton and her supporters seized upon the death of Glenda Rutherford to make their point forcefully about the problems surrounding St Mary's. The death of Josh Holdsworth, and the disappearance of Albert Macklin and the vicar, they argued in interviews with the media in a carefully orchestrated protest outside the church, illustrated the folly of allowing the hostel to operate. They demanded it be closed immediately, something about which Blizzard was asked when he arrived at the church shortly after 9.30. In an interview with a local radio reporter, he gave the impression that he agreed that the future of the hostel should be reviewed as a matter or urgency. The interview was broadcast at ten o'clock. The call to Blizzard's mobile came at 10.10 and by 10.30 he was sitting in Arthur Ronald's office, confronted by an uncomfortable chief superintendent and a furious borough councillor.

John Blizzard knew Aidan Gallagher well. They had frequently clashed swords in the past. Aidan Gallagher was a serious man, abandoned at birth, Blizzard always said, by his sense of humour. Now aged thirty-five, Gallagher was a professional sociologist, university-educated and full of ideals and jargon. A slim man with a thin face, short brown hair and a neatly trimmed brown beard, he sat in the office in his normal attire of brown cords and a brown cord jacket with patched elbows, over a black T-shirt with the words 'judge others as you would wish to be judged yourself'. It summed up Gallagher's approach to life, one which had helped him gain the council cabinet portfolio for social services when the Liberal Democrats had swept aside Labour after thirty-five years in power, at the last local elections. It was a stunning victory which grabbed national headlines and Gallagher was one of the councillors who gave plenty of interviews, appearing to enjoy basking in the glory.

The social services portfolio was a task which he approached with gusto. Within eight months of his arrival, the director and deputy director of social services had taken early retirement and a more liberal regime had been introduced. Allowing the St Mary's hostel to go ahead was one of the decisions which illustrated the enlightened approach but one which, oddly enough, had been passed behind closed doors by the council. There had been some local protests but the hostel had, until the unfortunate events of the past week, attracted precious little media attention beyond Hafton. Councillor Gallagher's presence in Ronald's office was because he tended to see any criticism of the hostel as a criticism of himself so he had reacted quickly to Blizzard's comments on the radio. But it was more than that: Gallagher detested Blizzard and his hard-line approach to crime and criminals and they had disagreed publicly on several occasions when the chief inspector made his views known at public forums. What irritated Gallagher even more was that such comments were usually greeted with enthusiastic applause from the floor, many members of the audience sharing Blizzard's view that the only way to stop crime was to stop criminals and if that meant longer prison sentences then so be it. The chief inspector, for his part, had no time for the councillor, having said to Colley on several occasions that 'the lunatics have taken over the asylum'.

Sitting in his office in City Hall that morning, Gallagher had listened to Blizzard's radio interview with a mixture of horror and delight, angered by the comments but immediately recognizing in them the chance to rid himself of a persistent thorn in his flesh. The disagreement had turned deeply personal for the councillor and now he was on the attack; this was the kind of opportunity not to be missed.

'I demand,' he said in that nasally voice of his, 'that this officer be removed from this inquiry immediately. It is clear that—'

'It is clear,' interrupted Ronald, torn between having to play the political game and a powerful impulse to slap the councillor, 'that we need an experienced police officer to deal with a serious situation like this.'

'Maybe,' replied Gallagher, then pointed at Blizzard. 'But not this clown, I would suggest.'

'Chief Inspector Blizzard is a highly competent officer,' snapped Ronald, 'and I will thank you not to tell me how to run my inquiries. I don't tell you how to run social services.'

The moment he had uttered the words, he realized his mistake. Gallagher's eyes gleamed and Ronald tried to not to show that he had slipped up.

'But he does,' said the councillor, pointing

once more at the chief inspector who was listening with a bored expression on his face. 'He said on radio that we were wrong to let the hostel go ahead.'

'Actually,' drawled Blizzard, speaking for the first time, 'what I said was that perhaps a review was required. I suspect a lot of people would agree with that.'

'Yes, but those kinds of decisions are for the experts and not a police officer,' retorted Gallagher. 'And from what I hear from Mr Rose-Harvey you have made no secret of your desire to see the hostel closed down.'

'So much for partnership,' muttered Blizzard.

'I admit,' said Ronald carefully, glaring at his colleague, 'that his comments may have been slightly misguided.'

'Misguided!' exclaimed Gallagher angrily 'He directly criticized a council decision! One that I personally recommended.'

'I was asked an honest question,' said Blizzard, 'and I gave an honest answer.'

'Yes, well, I am sure your Assistant Chief Constable Brown will not like that,' said Gallagher waspishly.

Blizzard allowed himself an ironic smile. Brown was a career uniformed police officer, fast-tracked through Bramshill, having spent precious little time on the streets, and appointed by the force several months before. As figurehead for the force's community safety strategy, he was forever popping up on the television to spout forth on the subject and had made no secret that he disliked officers like Blizzard, whom he believed had not moved with the times. Blizzard had met him twice in meetings. Neither meeting had gone well, Brown talking endlessly in sentences which never seemed to finish, Blizzard asking pointedly when the force was going to nick some villains.

Ronald sighed. Mention of Brown's name always meant trouble. Inwardly, he cursed Blizzard although, if he were brutally honest, he heartily agreed with the chief inspector's views.

'So is your chief inspector going to apologize?' asked Gallagher, breaking into the superintendent's reverie.

'I am sure that in future he will be more circumspect in his comments to the media,' replied Ronald, looking hopefully at his friend.

Noting his discomfort, and having no intention to apologize to anyone, Blizzard decided to play the game and nodded.

'I'll be more careful,' he said.

'But what about an apology—?' demanded Gallagher.

'I shouldn't push your luck,' said Ronald, silencing him with a sharp look.

'And another thing,' said the councillor. 'I understand that you and your colleagues are investigating these ridiculous stories about a sex ring in the city?'

'And what exactly makes you think that?' asked Ronald, feigning lack of concern.

'Well, let's just say I have contacts,' replied Gallagher evasively.

'Well, let's just say that they are wrong then, shall we?' replied Ronald. 'Because, there is no such inquiry. Am I making myself clear?'

'Well, I don't kn—'

'Am I making myself clear?' asked Ronald again, the tone of his voice transformed into the one which revealed the steel beneath his affable, diplomatic exterior.

The councillor hesitated for a moment, seemed about to reply then thought better of it and nodded.

'Well, if that will be all then, Mr Gallagher,' said Ronald briskly, standing up. 'I am a busy man.'

'That's Councillor Gallagher,' he replied archly, as the superintendent led him from the office and towards the front reception. *'Councillor* Gallagher.'

'Councillor spelled pillock,' Blizzard murmured, as he heard Ronald saying in the tone of voice normally reserved for distressed small children, 'My mistake, I do apologize.'

Blizzard roared with laughter then clapped a hand to his mouth lest the councillor hear from down the corridor. The chief inspector jumped to his feet and scuttled quickly from the office. He did not want to be there when

Arthur Ronald returned. They might be good friends but he was still the senior officer and whenever Blizzard stepped over the line, Ronald made sure he knew it. Besides, Blizzard had much to ponder. How, he asked himself, did the councillor know about what was supposed to be a covert inquiry? Back in his own office, he had just sat down when Colley limped in.

'I thought the doctor said you should have a day off,' commented Blizzard, looking up in surprise and eying the heavily bandaged right hand.

'I thought you might need me,' said the sergeant, sitting down.

'Yeah, it's strange, we are always short of one-armed, one-legged officers,' replied Blizzard sardonically. 'Something to do with equal opportunities.'

'Why thank you. Er, did I see the super escorting our Mr Gallagher out of the building just now?'

'That's *Councillor* Gallagher,' Blizzard corrected him.

'I take it you are in trouble again?'

'No, in fact, he came in to suggest that I be promoted to deputy chief constable immediately.'

'Of course he did. What have you done this time?'

'I suggested in a radio interview that the future of the hostel should be reviewed.'

'Well, something needs to happen,' said Colley. 'I have just been up to the church and there is a massive media scrum up there. With Margaret Hatton in her element.'

'I don't like her. Can't help feeling she is using the likes of Bob Maddox to get her face on the telly.'

'She did lose a son, though,' pointed out Colley, shifting his position in the chair to ease the pain in his throbbing knee.

'Yes, I know,' nodded Blizzard then leaned forward conspiratorially. 'Gallagher knows about Keeper.'

'Jesus.' Colley gave a low whistle. 'How?'

'How indeed.'

'There's something else,' said the sergeant. 'I have some interesting background information which our Mr Rose-Harvey did not tell us about.'

'Go on.'

'Well, I was sifting through the files in the vicar's office like you suggested, and I found this.' He fished a brown envelope from his jacket pocket and handed it over to the chief inspector.

'Now that is interesting,' breathed Blizzard, quickly scanning the contents, which comprised a hospital appointment for a mental outpatient unit in the city.

'Yeah, so I contacted the specialist whose name is at the bottom of the letter. Turns out the vicar has a long history of mental illness and the recent pressures with the takeover of the church had brought it all to the surface again. The specialist wasn't happy about talking but I persuaded him to tell me that Henry Sanders first went mad when he was in his late teens and living in Shrewsbury.'

'That's Shrewsbury for you,' said Blizzard sardonically.

'Yeah, but once a nutter always a nutter,' responded Colley sagely.

Blizzard raised a quizzical eyebrow.

'What?' asked Colley.

'You'd better not let the councillor hear you talking like that,' chuckled Blizzard, hauling himself from the chair and heading for the door. 'Come on, I think I need to get out of the building before Arthur pops in to discuss the finer points of social welfare policy'

Grinning despite the pain from his knee, Colley hobbled out of the office behind him, chuckling when he saw Blizzard turn left down the corridor then do a rapid about turn and head the other way with quick steps as Ronald appeared. As they entered the car park, Blizzard's mobile phone rang.

'You owe me one,' said the disembodied voice.

'You know,' replied Blizzard with a smile, 'I think you may be right, Arthur.'

CHAPTER TWENTY-THREE

By Friday night, the pressure was growing on the police as the local evening newspaper was packed with news about the investigation, none of it good. There is nothing like crime to sell papers and the reporters had taken full advantage of the situation. There was a front page lead about the lack of progress on the Glenda Rutherford inquiry with a second piece about the release without charge of Steve Holdsworth, who announced that he would be suing for wrongful arrest. The eloquent nature of the quotes led Blizzard to suspect that they had been largely made up by the reporter. The article certainly made Steve Holdsworth appear more intelligent than he was.

His release had come after he made a full confession to the detectives about his affair and eventually Blizzard was satisfied that an early theory that the father had killed the son to silence him over his assaults on the teenager was far off the mark. The realization disappointed him—he was desperate to see Holdsworth punished for his cruelty—but the professional officer in him persuaded Blizzard that releasing him was the only option. Ronald had been disappointed, too—a charge over the murder of Josh Holdsworth would have gone some way to easing the pressure on him.

On an inside page of the newspaper was a lengthy leader written by the editor—a former national newspaperman who had moved to the provinces on the offer of the top job and who was a long-time critic of the local police. He had argued for some time in his editorials that the force was losing the battle against crime and had seized on the incidents at St Mary's to reinforce his argument that they had no control over the situation. Such comments meant little to Blizzard but the article had a more pronounced effect on others, though, the chief constable issuing a stern rebuttal of the claims then bending Ronald's ear in a half-hour telephone call.

Adding to the pressure was a story about the latest assault on the church. Recent days had seen an escalating campaign to close the hostel, including three attacks with spray cans and a couple of smashed windows. The increasing severity of the attacks had led Blizzard to re-evaluate his theories and return to his initial gut instinct. What, he had asked Colley that morning as they sat in his office, if it was all very straightforward after all, that someone simply wanted them to think that the vicar was responsible in some way? What if, he had thought aloud, the real culprit was to be found among the mob angry at the way the church had gone out of its way to help Albert Macklin? It was such a train of thought which had led the detectives to a major decision, one which they had discussed fully with an uneasy Arthur Ronald, uneasy because of the potential public relations difficulties which it presented. There was no alternative, Blizzard said, to pulling in some of the key protestors, starting with Margaret Hatton and Bob Maddox again. The former, it emerged, had gone to London for a meeting, the latter had, it appeared, vanished into thin air.

It did not take the officers long to pick up the trail—a visit to the Harry's Arms by Blizzard and Colley and a few veiled threats to the assembled drinkers had sorted the problem. Had the evening newspaper editor been sitting in the packed briefing room at Abbey Road Police Station shortly after eight that night, he would perhaps have been more circumspect about what he was writing because if there was one thing that bonded John Blizzard and Arthur Ronald, it was their dislike of inaction. They believed that to win the fight against crime, the police had to be constantly running operations to transfer the fear from the victims to the criminals. Such thinking might have become trendy modern speak within the force—the media-friendly chief constable was constantly stressing it as a theme—but Blizzard, Ronald and their ilk had been doing it for years. And there were plenty of villains who lived in fear of a knock on their door from Blizzard or one of his team.

Now, as Ronald stood at the front of the briefing room and surveyed his troops, he reflected with satisfaction that there were going to be plenty of knocks on doors that night. This was what it was about: hitting the villains where it hurt, not placating them. Before him were more than seventy officers, lounging about on the chairs, chatting casually, swapping stories and exchanging jokes, some of them drafted in from other areas of the county and renewing old acquaintances amid plenty of laughter and back slapping. Most were in uniform, some wore plainclothes and a number—burly officers, hard men—were in the dark-blue overalls and caps which identified them as the operational support team, the heavy hitters brought in as foot soldiers on the tough jobs. Also scattered among them were officers from the armed response unit requested specifically by Ronald given the nature of the target that night. One or two were eating sandwiches, the short notice with which they had been called in robbing them of a hot meal, others were chewing on chocolate bars or swigging from bottles of water. But no one complained: they had seen the newspaper articles as well and were determined to do something which would prove to the villains of the city that the police were in charge.

Standing next to the superintendent at the front of the room was John Blizzard, clearly enjoying himself. Colley always said that these were the kinds of situations when Blizzard truly came into his own, when the game was afoot and he had been given the resources to make sure that the police won it. John Blizzard believed in kicking in doors and locking up villains. Restorative justice to him meant replacing the doorframe afterwards. His hardline stance made him unpopular with some of his superiors but hugely popular with the rank and file who spent their days on the streets, constantly confronted by cocky young criminals and frustrated members of the public, and equally angered themselves by what they saw as a criminal justice service gone soft.

The reason for the gathering that night was a hushed conversation which David Colley had had with a contact earlier in the day. The homeless man, who was often seen begging on the high street, was also a police informer, the sergeant slipping him a few quid here and there in return for information. Chaz—only Ronald and Blizzard at Abbey Road knew his real identity—had been a secondary school teacher but a mental breakdown following a series of assaults by pupils left him stressed out and unsuitable for the job. Forced to resign at the age of thirty-one and with his marriage over, his life had fallen apart and he now found himself living on the street, the Salvation Army hostel offering him a bed for the night and a warm meal. Other accommodation had been offered at Her Majesty's pleasure, a short spell for theft.

When he was not in prison, his time was spent begging, few of his former students and colleagues able to recognize him through the straggly beard and unkempt appearance. One who did was Colley's girlfriend, Jay, who had known Chaz when he was a primary school teacher before he made the move to the comprehensive. In those days he had been bright-eyed, idealistic and full of great expectations, but three years in the tough secondary school had broken him and an incident in which a six-foot teenager had struck him with a chair, resulting in three days in hospital, had proved the final straw.

Jay had recognized him when she and Colley had been shopping in the city centre one Saturday morning and, horrified and embarrassed in equal measure, she had given him some money. Over the months that followed, Chaz had repaid the generosity with a stream of low-level tip-offs for the sergeant, culminating in one which elevated him to the next level of informant, leading to the arrest of a man running a group of prostitutes, something which had impressed, if grudgingly, Alex Mather and the vice squad who had been after him for the best part of a year. Over the two years that followed, Chaz had kept the information coming, leading to more arrests which had significantly enhanced the sergeant's reputation.

But this call had been different: Chaz, who normally welcomed their meetings and the money that they provided, was clearly terrified and insisted that Colley meet him in a local park rather than their usual city centre pub. Colley must not approach him, said Chaz, so, as agreed, Colley sat on a bench pretending to read a newspaper and Chaz hid in a bush and whispered his information. Although Colley could not see him, he recognized the fear in his informant's voice.

'I hear you're after Maddox,' Chaz had begun.

'How do you know?' asked the surprised sergeant.

They were indeed after Bob Maddox. With David Reed hovering between life and death, Blizzard, weary of the blatant deceit shown by just about everyone the detectives encountered, had declared that it was time to shake some of the secrets loose and Bob Maddox was one of his main targets. However, Danny's father had gone to ground and several visits to his house had elicited no information as to his whereabouts. Not even his associates knew—or were prepared to say—where he was, however dire the threats.

'Am I right?' asked Chaz.

'As always,' admitted Colley. 'How do you know?'

'People are talking about it.'

'People?'

'On The Spur.'

'Is that where he is?' asked Colley.

'Yes'

'Where?'

'Can't tell you that.'

'It's a big estate,' remarked Colley.

'You'll find him.'

'How do you know where he is?'

'He's my heroin supplier.'

'Jesus, Chaz,' exclaimed Colley, turning round and peering into the darkness at the scared face, 'I thought you said you were clean again!'

'Do you want this information or not?' and the voice had a sharp edge. 'I'm out on a limb over this. If they get hold of me, I'm dead meat.'

'Go on.'

'If you want Maddox,' said the voice, 'keep an eye on Lavender House. They're dealing the drugs out of there. He's one of the big fish.'

'Will he be there now?'

'Yeah, he's been in the flat ever since word got out that you were after him.'

'Thanks.'

'Worth a few quid?' asked Chaz hopefully.

'As long as it doesn't go on drugs.'

There was a pause.

'Chaz?'

'I want to come off the drugs,' said the disembodied voice. 'Honest, Dave.'

'In which case,' said the sergeant. 'I have a little proposition for you. Do it right and I'll sort you some rehab.'

Over the next couple of minutes he outlined his plan.

'OK, Dave, I'll do it,' said the voice.

'Good man. Do you need anything else?'

But with a rustle of leaves Chaz was away. Colley had returned to Abbey Road and reported his information to Blizzard, who had immediately consulted Ronald. The three of them had locked themselves away for an hour before emerging to announce that they were prepared to mount a raid as long as they could confirm that Maddox was there. The sergeant took a couple of officers and mounted a covert observation, confirming by late-afternoon that Maddox was in one of the top floor flats in the Lavender House block. Whoever named those blocks had a warped sense of humour, Colley concluded, although lavender would have been nice to remove the smell of stale urine from the stairwell, he thought.

After making his decision, Ronald had informed the Chief Constable, who was delighted that something was happening, and the operation was duly sanctioned. The reason the decision had to go so far up the line of command was that The Spur—or more properly The Larkspur, named after one of

175

the eighteenth-century fighting ships that used to sail from Hafton—was a major troublespot. Built in the heart of the western division in the '60s, it was a rundown place, decades of council neglect, exacerbated by lack of investment, having allowed it to deteriorate. Once-smart blocks of flats had increasingly been turned over to low-level criminals, the decent tenants often forced out by threats and violence, and the estate quickly becoming a major centre for drug dealing.

The police knew all about it and mounted regular raids, but six months before, one of the operations had gone horribly wrong. Two uniformed officers on a routine inquiry, relating to a stolen car, had called at a flat and were greeted with a hail of abuse from within. During the scuffle that followed, a 19-year-old drug addict had died. That the post-mortem had concluded he was already ill with hepatitis and could have died at any time, mattered not to the criminals who ran The Spur. They did not care about the addict, of course, but they did recognize a golden opportunity to cause trouble and persuaded the man's family to demand a public inquiry into the death, a campaign they had continued even though the official investigation into the incident exonerated the police. The result had been a reluctance among local police commanders to do anything which might inflame the situation—and that suited the drug dealers perfectly.

It had not suited Arthur Ronald and John Blizzard and they were desperate for action. However, it was not that simple. The Spur had become extremely tense and whenever officers went onto the estate, they went in numbers and were usually greeted with violence, bricks hurled from upper balconies, foul abuse and crowds of hooded young men appearing from the shadows within seconds, often armed with knives and wooden staves. So concerned did the chief constable become that he ordered a softly-softly approach, a situation which had frustrated Ronald and Blizzard even more, their determination to act increased by the regular calls for action from the association set up to represent the few honest tenants who remained, living in their cocoons of fear. Only the fact that Bob Maddox was linked to the murder inquiry had persuaded the chief constable to sanction the operation.

Once Maddox's presence had been confirmed and approval had been granted, Blizzard had put in a quick call to the Drugs Squad and together they had planned a major raid. This was no longer just about Maddox, this was an opportunity to take out a whole line of command in the city's drugs world. The squad were delighted despite the short notice. They had also become increasingly frustrated at what they saw as the lack of backing for their proposal to mount such a raid and were pleased when Blizzard and Ronald said they could use Maddox as the excuse to go in heavy. Teams were rapidly assembled from across the city and the Drugs Squad identified a number of flats that they wanted to target. They had also heard that Bob Maddox was involved and Colley's observations meant his flat was added to the list.

The relaxed atmosphere changed as Blizzard clapped his hands and called for quiet. Suddenly, all eyes were on him.

'Ladies and gentlemen,' he said, 'thank you for gathering at such short notice. Your presence here confirms what I have always known about the men and women of this force—that the promise of overtime works wonders.'

There was a murmur of laughter round the room, momentarily easing the tension. Colley, leaning against a wall at the back, allowed himself a chuckle: seeing Blizzard deal with the troops was always an education. They might not find him an easy person to get to know—Blizzard did not let many people get close—but to a man and woman, the officers respected and trusted him. And when he addressed such gatherings, there was some-thing about the way he spoke, a fire which inspired those who listened with a burning desire to get the job done and done right.

Now, they recognized that steely expression and the hardening of his voice as he paced around the front of the room.

'This will not be an easy operation,' he continued. 'Bob Maddox is our main target—we want him in connection with the death of Josh Holdsworth—but the Drugs Squad have identified a number of other properties. You should all have the list by now. I do not need to tell you that The Spur is not an easy place to work and I want this done properly. I want the drug dealers to realize that we do not believe in no-go areas in this division. I want the doors to go in if that is what it takes. If we get this right, it will put the fear of God into the lot of them.'

He smiled. 'And after the week I've had, I can tell you that I am already terrified of the big fella.'

More laughter. Then Blizzard was serious again. 'So let's take them out.'

There was a murmur of agreement.

'As you will have noticed,' continued the chief inspector, 'we have some visitors. You will recognize the firearms unit. They're the one with the big weapons.'

A few lewd sniggers. The firearms team feigned offence but secretly everyone knew they loved the kudos that came with their job.

'And the Drugs Squad.' Blizzard nodded to several plainclothes officers in the corner. 'See them later for spliffs.'

More laughter.

'But listen,' said Blizzard, not laughing now,

179

the mixture of humour and gravity a beguiling and powerful combination, 'I want us to be careful out there tonight. There are some nasty characters on The Spur but remember, we are the police, *we* run this city, not them, and it is time to remind them of that.'

One or two officers applauded, Ronald nodded his appreciation and there was a heightened energy in the room as the officers stood up and headed for the door. They were ready to do battle. Twenty minutes later, the crew buses and cars swung out of the police station car park. Command of the operation on the ground had been handed over to uniformed chief inspector Gerry Craven, a tough no-nonsense officer with twenty years' experience. Swiftly he organized the teams and moments later, they were heading through the night into the estate.

The Spur had been constructed around three large quadrangles, bordered on all sides by flats. Broken glass littered the quadrangles and weeds poked through the cracks in the concrete. The blocks themselves were dilapidated, the concrete crumbling, the paintwork peeling, those doors which had not been kicked in splintered and bearing ugly gashes. Many of the windows were smashed and the remaining ones were grimy. Many had been boarded up and graffiti had been scrawled across them. It was a terrible place, thought Blizzard, as he stood silently in one of the quadrangles and gazed around at the blocks, illuminated by a full moon clearly visible in the scudding clouds above.

'Time someone bulldozed these,' he said to Colley, who was standing next to him.

The sergeant nodded. 'It's certainly a God-forsaken place,' he said.

'Mind you, so is St Mary's,' grunted Blizzard.

Moments later the police teams were moving in. There was a lot of shouting and thumping and the sound of doors being kicked in by the raiding parties.

'Go on,' said Blizzard, noticing his sergeant's gleaming eyes.

Colley shot him a grateful look and limped off across the square and up one of the stinking, dark stairwells, rugby injury and damaged hand seemingly forgotten. Moments later, Blizzard saw him plunge into one of the flats and manhandle a protesting man out onto the landing. The chief inspector chuckled.

'Kids,' he said.

'Should he be doing that with that hand of his?' asked Ronald, ambling up and following his colleague's gaze to where Colley was handcuffing the man before handing him over to one of the uniforms and plunging back into the darkness, 'I mean, what about Health and Safety and all that?'

'You do spout some rubbish,' grunted Blizzard affectionately. 'Besides, you try telling him.'

'Aye, maybe you're right.'

Moments later, their mood changed as a loud crack reverberated around the estate. Within seconds, the firearms team was sprinting up the stairwell of one of the blocks, followed by Blizzard, and struggling to keep up, a huffing Ronald. Blizzard reached the middle landing where a wild-eyed man was staggering about and wielding a handgun. Aged in his mid-twenties, he was dressed only in jeans, his bare, tattooed torso revealing the almost skeletal frame of the heroin addict. Chief Inspector Craven and the leader of the firearms team, crouched at the end of the landing nearest to Blizzard, gestured frantically for Blizzard to get back and he and the superintendent, who was struggling up the stairs, waited in the inky darkness, unable to see what was happening but listening to the gunman's wild threats and aware of every heartbeat as they heard the inspector order the man to put down his weapon. A moment's silence then the order was repeated. Then a loud blast. Blizzard poked his head round the corner and could see the man lying on the floor, blood oozing from a gaping wound in his chest, legs twisted sickeningly beneath him. Standing a few metres away was one of the firearms team, gun in hand, firm of stance.

'Shit,' breathed Blizzard, walking out onto the landing.

'He aimed it at me,' said the officer, turning round. 'No option, sir.'

'He's right,' nodded Chief Inspector Craven.

Blizzard nodded. Ronald stood behind him, ashen-faced, not from what he was witnessing—he had seen enough dead bodies in his time—but at the thought of the flak which would come his way. The chief constable, he knew, was a man whose failure to support his officers was legendary and who would, no doubt, conveniently forget that he had authorized the operation in the first place. Glancing over the balustrade, Ronald saw officers and their handcuffed prisoners down below staring up in horror after the exchange of gunfire.

'Not exactly the result I had hoped for,' he murmured.

'Oh, I dunno,' said Blizzard casually, wandering over to join him and leaning on the parapet. 'It'll put the willies up the dealers.'

'Yes, well, I'd rather you didn't say that to the media,' said Ronald darkly.

Blizzard watched him go in grim silence. His radio crackled.

'Sorry, sir,' said Colley. 'No Bob Maddox.'

'Brilliant,' breathed Blizzard, spotting his sergeant leading someone out of the shadows at the far end of the quadrangle down below. 'Who's your little pal then?'

'I was wrong,' and Colley, waving a

183

bandaged hand at him. 'it isn't a God-forsaken place.'

'Who is it?' asked the chief inspector, peering across the square.

'The Good Lord's emissary on Earth!'

Blizzard stared down at the bedraggled Reverend Henry Sanders and a beam spread across his face.

'Now that,' he said happily, 'is more like it.'

CHAPTER TWENTY-FOUR

The scene at Abbey Road Police Station that Saturday morning was a distinct irritant to John Blizzard. News of the shooting had broken overnight and, predictably, the media had descended on the station, Blizzard having to edge his car through a scrum of reporters and film crews when he arrived for work. The official inquiry team was already there as always happened with firearms deaths, as was the chief constable and an uncomfortable-looking Arthur Ronald. Not only was the media coverage already hugely negative, but one of the radio stations had run a story revealing that Bob Maddox was the reason for the raid in the first place and Margaret Hatton, standing in front of the police station, had given an interview saying how terrible it was that the bereaved father of a child should be treated in such a way. Blizzard had snorted when he heard her words.

Blizzard had hoped to conduct an interview with Henry Sanders early in the morning but that plan was frustrated when he was ordered to attend an initial interview with the inquiry team. He had to sit outside the interview-room for an hour then spend a further hour with the investigators, recounting everything leading up to the shooting, repeating it several times for the stern-faced officers, forced to justify his reasoning for supporting an operation in such a dangerous place. As someone who had been required to submit to several such interviews in his time, he did not enjoy the experience but acknowledged that the detectives had a job to do. Not everyone felt that way: anyone from complaints was frozen out by many officers, but Blizzard always co-operated fully whenever called in for questioning. Besides, he regarded it as useful in a strange way because it allowed him to analyse his responses and emotions under the pressure of their questions and to better understand the ways in which he could exert a similar pressure on suspects in his own interviews. Nevertheless, after an hour, and not in a particularly good mood because of the time lost, he emerged from the stuffy room and headed back to his office, where he found David Colley.

'How'd it go?' asked the sergeant, glancing up from the newspaper he was reading.

185

'Usual stuff,' said Blizzard. 'I can't see that there's a problem really, the guy had already fired once and was pointing his gun at Eddie Makin. What else could he do?'

'That's the feeling among the troops,' nodded Colley.

'Besides,' said Blizzard, sitting down behind his desk and glancing at the growing pile of paperwork. 'It's one less druggie to worry about.'

'I assume you didn't say that to the inquiry team?' smiled Colley.

'Give me some credit,' grunted Blizzard. 'Anyway, time for some proper police work. I think we need to interview the good reverend.'

'Not just yet,' said Colley, 'Margaret Hatton is waiting in front reception.'

'I wonder what she wants?' said Blizzard, intrigued. 'Go and get her, will you?'

Colley left the room, little sign of the limp, and as he disappeared, Blizzard shouted after him, 'Dave!'

The sergeant popped his head back round the door.

'You're not planning to play rugby this afternoon?'

'Well,' replied the sergeant, 'the doc says I should rest my hand for at least three days, and my knee still hurts.'

'So what time are you kicking off?' smiled Blizzard.

'Two thirty.'

'We'll get the vicar done by then,' nodded Blizzard. 'After all, I'd hate to deprive you of the chance to break your neck! Or anyone else's for that matter.'

'Thanks,' grinned Colley and loped off to get Margaret Hatton, leaving the chief inspector shaking his head at the madness of it all.

Five minutes later, the file read, he was sitting opposite a very different Margaret Hatton. The sharp business suit, deep blue this morning, was still there, the hair was as immaculate as ever and the make-up had been applied perfectly as usual, but the expression on the face was different. There were bags beneath eyes which seemed strangely haunted.

'And what brings you here, Mrs Hatton?' asked Blizzard coolly, noting the change in her demeanour and relishing the chance to enjoy the upper hand for the first time in his dealings with her.

'I need help,' she said in a quiet voice, obviously hating having to ask the chief inspector for his assistance.

'Would you like me to invite a camera crew or two in here to film our meeting?' asked Blizzard drily.

She shook her head.

'I've received death threats,' she said hoarsely.

'Really?' replied Blizzard, straightening up in his chair, his interest well and truly engaged.

'Do tell me more.'

'You must be enjoying this,' she said bitterly.

'Actually I'm not,' said the chief inspector.

'We might have our disagreements but I don't like people being threatened on our manor.'

'The first one came two nights ago,' she said, grateful to unburden herself, the words coming in a rush. 'Hotel reception patched a call through to my room at eleven o'clock. It was a man's voice. I didn't recognize it. He said he had seen my television interview that evening . . .'

'Refresh my memory, there have been so many,' said Blizzard sardonically.

She glared at him, regaining some composure.

'The one where I said it was time that paedophiles were driven from the city,' she said icily.

'Oh, *that* one,' remarked Blizzard. 'Do I take it your caller did not share your views on social justice?'

'He said that if I said anything else, something horrible would happen to me.'

'Which doubtless you ignored?'

She nodded.

'I gave an interview with local radio yesterday, saying the same thing.'

'And he called again?'

She nodded, clearly under great strain, composure crumbling once more. The lips were quivering slightly, and the detectives thought she was perhaps close to tears.

'The call came at eleven-thirty. He said I had been warned and that if I did not leave the city today, I would be killed.'

'And will you?'

'No!' The reply was vehement.

'Why?'

'There is work to be done here. As long as that hostel stays open—'

'I understand its future is under review,' said Blizzard, glancing at Colley who nodded. 'Apparently the good Councillor Gallagher is holding a meeting next week to discuss its future.'

'I didn't know that.'

She sounded surprised.

'Indeed,' said Blizzard. 'So, these death threats, any idea who they might have come from?'

'It could be a paedophile.'

'Possible,' nodded the chief inspector.

'Or someone from the church.'

'Also possible,' agreed Blizzard. 'Let me be honest with you, Mrs Hatton, your media campaign has made life very difficult for me and my team. It has stirred up strong emotions. How the hell can we conduct our inquiries if everywhere we go there are people waving placards and specially invited reporters sticking their noses in?'

'The public has a right to know.'

'Yes,' snapped Blizzard. 'But not if it jeopardizes one of my operations. I have a good mind to charge you with perverting the course of justice.'

'On what grounds?' she exclaimed, outraged at the suggestion.

'Well,' said Blizzard coldly, 'someone tipped off the media that we were looking for Bob Maddox last night. According to a couple of the drug dealers we interviewed, he scarpered when he received a phone call a few minutes before we arrived on the estate. Then, lo and behold, there is a radio report this morning saying that our friend Bob was the target of the raid.'

'It could have come from anyone,' she said uncomfortably.

'Yes, but it came from you,' said Blizzard, nodding at Colley. 'Tell her, Sergeant.'

'I know the radio reporter,' explained Colley. 'We went to school together. I rang him this morning and he told me you tipped off Maddox that we were looking for him.'

She went white.

'And I would love to know how you knew,' said Blizzard.

'Ah, well, I can answer that one as well,' said Colley. 'The reporter claims you went round to visit Bob Maddox yesterday evening about the latest protest but turned back when you spotted our surveillance team parked nearby. The reporter says you contacted Mrs Maddox

190

to rearrange your meeting and told her the police were outside.'

'And I reckon,' said Blizzard, 'that she rang her husband, giving him time to slip out of the estate before we arrived.'

Margaret Hatton opened and closed her mouth several times but words would not come.

'And if I can make that stick, I am sure the CPS would happily take the prosecution on,' concluded the chief inspector.

Margaret Hatton slumped back into her chair and gazed at him weakly.

'I didn't mean any harm,' she whispered at length.

'But the media attention does serve your purpose perfectly,' said Blizzard.

'That hostel has to be closed,' she riposted. 'We have to drive padeophiles out of—'

'Yes but you're playing with fire, lady,' said Blizzard. 'There's nothing gets people going like paedophiles. Once you press that button anything can happen. You made a bad situation a thousand times worse. Let's hope it wasn't one of the protestors who attacked David Reed—'

'But I thought the vicar had been arrested for that,' she said in surprise. 'That's what people are saying.'

'Maybe they are,' replied Blizzard enigmatically, and gestured to his sergeant to take her away. 'But all is not always as it seems . . .'

CHAPTER TWENTY-FIVE

It was a different Henry Sanders who faced them in the interview room at Abbey Room shortly before lunchtime. They had expected a broken man but he had dug deep into his reserves and had staged a remarkable recovery, particularly given what he had been through over recent days. One of the search teams had discovered the reverend locked in a filthy, squalid ground-floor flat at The Spur, sprawled among old newspapers, burger boxes and empty beer cans, his hands tied to a radiator. He had not eaten or drunk for thirty-six hours and the medical examiner had confirmed that in addition to dehydration, he had been the victim of a vicious assault—probably several of them—diagnosing a broken nose, three chipped teeth and a couple of cracked ribs.

After being taken to hospital for a check-up, the vicar had been brought back to the station and taken to the interview room which the detectives were now approaching. Expecting to find a cowed figure sitting at the table, they were surprised at what they saw. Sanders' relief at being freed—fuelled by the knowledge that his time skulking in the shadows, glancing fearfully over his shoulder, had come to an end—had given him strength and he seemed somehow taller, more upright in his chair. There was fire in his eyes, albeit they were badly bruised, and a determined expression on his battered face. Henry Sanders had stopped running and it felt good. His ordeal in the empty flat had given him time to reflect and had allowed him to renew his faith. Now, he was ready to face his accusers and looked up as Blizzard and Colley entered the windowless little room, which was illuminated by a single dim lightbulb.

'Henry, Henry,' sighed the chief inspector sitting down wearily and opening a file. 'For a man of the cloth you seem to have a strange idea of goodness.'

'We are all sinners,' replied the vicar calmly.

'Yes,' nodded Blizzard, 'but few seem to make such a career out of it. Your previous church seemed to think that you stole money from them—and Edgar Rose-Harvey would dearly like to have his twenty-eight thousand back.'

'That man!' spat the vicar through his chipped teeth and swollen lips.

'Indeed,' said Blizzard, noting that it was not the first time such words had been used to describe the church leader. 'So let's start at the beginning, shall we? Before you tell us why someone decided to turn you into a punchbag, you should be aware that we know about you and Marian . . .'

The vicar started, the first crack in his freshly constructed composure showing.

'There's nothing to know,' he said defensively, but it did not sound convincing.

'Stealing, adultery, lying,' replied the chief inspector casually 'You certainly do run through the sins, Henry.'

His voice suddenly turned harsh and there was an icy glare in his eyes.

'But it's time to cut the crap. I have enough problems without playing your stupid little games. Marian told us everything. Said you planned to run away together. I take it that was what the money was for?'

The vicar nodded humbly, startled, and not a little frightened, by the sudden change in Blizzard's demeanour, his confidence of a few moments ago evaporating.

'Did Josh know about your affair?' asked Colley, who was leaning against the wall.

Sanders nodded, grateful that he did not have to deal with the fearsome chief inspector.

'Did he approve?' asked the sergeant.

'He liked me,' said the vicar.

'Are you sure?' and Colley looked at him closely.

'What do you mean?' A look of outrage came over his face as he realized the direction in which the questioning was leading. Clearly, the sergeant was as tough as his boss.

'Just answer the question.'

'Yes, he did. He was a nice kid.'

'Why were you down on the canal path the day he was killed?' asked Colley.

'Now come on!' shouted Sanders, leaping angrily to his feet.

'Sit down!' snarled Blizzard. 'What my sergeant is saying is that perhaps Josh didn't like you, didn't like the idea of you running off with his mother, maybe he protested, maybe you attacked him.'

'Never! Never! Do you hear me? Never!' yelled the vicar, still on his feet.

'I hear you,' said Blizzard calmly, jabbing a finger at the chair as his voice hardened again. 'Now sit down! For what it's worth, I don't think you killed Josh Holdsworth.'

'But you just said . . .'

'I had to ask.'

Relief enveloped the vicar's face as he slumped back into his chair.

'I thank you for that,' he said gratefully.

'But I'm not sure about poor old Glenda Rutherford.'

Sanders stared at him in horror, the blood draining from his face.

'Or David Reed.'

'You surely don't think . . .' cried the vicar, almost as if the full enormity of his situation had only just hit home, his voice tailing off as he stared at them.

'Look at it from our point of view,' said Blizzard. 'We know that David Reed had

195

rumbled your fraud and that he confronted you in the hostel that night. And we know that the only other person who knew what was happening was Glenda Rutherford.'

'Yes, but—'

'You have been under a lot of stress, suddenly the one thing you wanted—to run away and start a new life with Marian—was threatened by what David knew. Maybe you lashed out, grabbed the first thing that came to hand.'

'No! No!'

Sanders was on his feet again.

'Sit down, dammit! It's like interviewing a sodding Jack-in-the Box.'

'You've got me wrong, I'm not like that,' moaned Sanders, sitting down heavily.

'We can all do anything if the pressure is too much for us,' persisted Blizzard, the tone accusing. 'Maybe you set out to silence Glenda as well because she was the only other person who could testify that you were at the hostel that night. After all, you had nothing to lose. The theft alone was enough to send you to prison. Maybe you simply stepped over the line, Mr Sanders.'

'You've got it all wrong,' protested the vicar. 'I could never hurt anyone.'

'And then there's your history of mental illness,' said Blizzard pointedly.

'That was a long time ago, for God's sake!'

'Yes, but you have been to see a consultant

lately, have you not?'

'Yes, yes. But I am not a violent man. Yes, I admit, I was angry when David Reed confronted me that night but I didn't attack him. What do you think I am?'

'I'm still trying to work it out,' said Blizzard drily. 'For all I know, you may be a cold-blooded killer.'

'Oh, for God's sake!'

'Funny,' murmured Blizzard. 'Whenever anyone mentions that name nasty things seem to happen to people.'

'You are wrong about me,' insisted Sanders. 'David gave me the opportunity to return the money and said he would not tell anyone. Then I left: I did not hit him.'

Blizzard leaned back in his chair and surveyed the vicar thoughtfully. 'I think I believe you,' he said at length.

'Thank God,' breathed the vicar.

'But why were you on the canal path?' asked Colley.

'I go for a walk there sometimes—helps clear my head.'

'OK,' said Blizzard. 'Tell me about Bob Maddox.'

Sanders sighed. 'They came to my house,' he said.

'Who did?'

'Maddox and his son. Grabbed me as I was walking up the drive to the vicarage and bundled me into a car.'

'What did they want with you?'

'Said they knew about me and Marian. Said Steve Holdsworth was furious.'

'How did Holdsworth know about the affair?' asked Colley.

'Maddox told him when he got home after Josh was killed.' The vicar's lips quivered as he mentioned the death of the teenager. 'It's no age to die is it?' he said, and turned moist eyes on the detectives.

'No, it's not, Mr Sanders,' said Blizzard, his tone a little gentler.

'It explains why Maddox wanted to meet Steve Holdsworth before he went home,' said Colley. 'Maddox probably knew the affair would all come out once we started poking around. Wanted to warn him.'

Blizzard nodded.

'So how come you ended up in the flat?' asked the sergeant.

'They took me to several places, kept hitting me, said Steve wanted to see me when you released him. Yesterday, they took me to that awful place.'

He shuddered at the memory.

'When your men kicked the door in I was convinced it was Steve,' and the vicar started to sob. 'I thought I was going to die.'

'OK, Henry,' said Blizzard, a touch of compassion in his voice. 'Here's what we are going to do. I don't think you killed Glenda or attacked David Reed but you will be charged with the theft of twenty-eight thousand pounds from the church.'

With a massive effort, Sanders stopped crying and nodded dumbly.

'You will be kept here until you appear in court on Monday. Frankly, I reckon this police station is just about the only place where you are safe right now. Apart from Maddox and his Neanderthal son, plenty of people out there want to have a go at you.'

'Because of the money?'

'Don't be so bloody naïve! Because they reckon you killed Glenda Rutherford and Josh Holdsworth!'

'But I didn't!' wailed Sanders, burying his head in his hands. 'How could they think that?'

'Because Margaret Hatton has got them in such a state they don't know what they are thinking,' said Blizzard. 'David will read you your rights in a minute. Do you understand?'

Another nod. The vicar seemed deflated; unburdening himself and being confronted with fresh horror after fresh horror had taken a massive amount out of him. Now he sat silently as Colley recited the words he had uttered so many times before.

Minutes later and in the corridor outside the interview-room, Blizzard leaned against the wall and closed his eyes.

'It's all very well nicking the vicar,' he said, 'but it doesn't get us anywhere nearer to finding out who killed Josh and Glenda or attacked David Reed, does it?'

''Fraid not,' said Colley, glancing at his watch.

'What time is it?' asked Blizzard quickly.

'Five past two.'

'You'll just make it,' said the chief inspector. 'Go on, get off to your match.'

'Are you sure?'

'Yes.' Blizzard gestured for his sergeant to go. 'I'll clear up here.'

He watched his sergeant scuttle off down the corridor. As he reached the end, Blizzard yelled.

'Oh, David?'

Colley wheeled round and gave him an enquiring look.

'Try to come back in one piece this time!'

Colley gave a cheery wave and disappeared round the corner. Blizzard watched him go, chuckled then pushed open the door to the interview-room.

'Now, Mr Sanders,' he said affably. 'Where were we?'

CHAPTER TWENTY-SIX

Sunday is usually regarded as a day of rest— but not if you worked for John Blizzard on a major inquiry. Despite the rigours, his team never objected to working the extra hours during such investigations because they knew the chief inspector was always scrupulously fair, either immediately signing off significant overtime payments—a practice which regularly landed him in trouble with the force's penny-pinching chief accountant—or authorizing plenty of time off when the circumstances allowed. He might not have been much of a family man himself but John Blizzard realized that officers needed time with wives, girlfriends and children to preserve body and soul. However, the other side to this approach was that when the chase was on, he expected total commitment from his detectives. And the chase was definitely on.

After Colley left for his rugby match, the chief inspector had completed the initial paperwork on Henry Sanders then headed off to see his aged mother, who lived in a local sheltered housing complex in the city. After wrapping her up in coat, gloves, scarf and hat—commenting that she looked like the granny in the Giles cartoons, an allusion which she did not appreciate—he had pushed her round the nearby park, making small talk on automatic pilot while allowing his mind to sift the evidence gathered over the past week. On their return to her flat, he tarried awhile over a cup of tea and the story he had heard a thousand times about the change in her medication then headed home for a quiet evening curled up on the sofa with a good book. John Blizzard might have spent his days and nights mired in real-life outrages but he was still an *aficionado* of classic crime novels and grabbed the chance to wallow in them whenever he could. Colleagues found the fact amazing; they tended to choose pastimes as far from police work as possible—Colley with his rugby, Tulley with his cello, Ramsay with his martial arts—but whether it be Wilkie Collins, Arthur Conan Doyle or Ellery Queen, Blizzard devoured them all. He always found it amusing that he never managed to solve the mystery before his fictional counterparts.

Shortly before ten, having dozed off on the sofa, woken as his book slipped off his lap and onto the floor, he had stumbled bleary-eyed up to bed and was asleep in minutes, unusual for him because it usually took at least an hour as his mind continued to race. He woke up ten hours later, feeling remarkably refreshed, the fatigue of the night before banished, energies which had been running low fully restored. John Blizzard felt a renewed vigour for the inquiry and after getting in early to Abbey Road Police Station, he spent an hour and a half sifting through paperwork. After nipping out for a coffee just after nine thirty, he had just sat down again and was eyeing the Post-it note on his computer with interest when Colley appeared at the door, sporting a black eye, a gashed cheek, a thick lip and with a fresh bandage on his injured hand. Despite all this, he looked equally refreshed.

'Bloody hell,' grunted Blizzard. 'It's a secondment from Zombie Patrol. I take it you played then?'

'Too right we did,' grinned Colley, sitting down and stretching out his legs. 'And we won—three-two.'

'I thought rugby matches usually had bigger scores than that?'

'I'm talking about players carried off on stretchers,' and the sergeant roared with laughter. 'God knows how Broughton will get any town centre patrols out today!'

Blizzard sighed, pretending to be irritated but the pretence was pretty blatant—deliberately so—and it was obvious to the sergeant that he had enjoyed the joke just as much.

'So where are we then?' asked Colley, once his laughter had subsided. 'I take it the vicar is still taking advantage of our hospitality?'

'Yeah. I checked earlier, he had a good night. Frankly, I think he's just pleased to be out of harm's way . . .'

'Oh, I dunno, have you tasted Rorky's tea?'

'Point taken,' smiled the chief inspector. 'Anyhow, I have asked the DI to tie up the inquiry into the missing money and get Henry Sanders to make a full statement. And Tulley is sticking with the other thing.'

'So what are we going to do?' asked the sergeant in surprise.

'We,' beamed Blizzard, glancing at his watch, leaping up, struggling in his jacket and grabbing the Post-it note, 'are going to church. But first, we have to make a hospital visit.'

'You're becoming quite pastoral in your old age,' replied Colley, following him out of the door. 'Why, you'll be doing the Bible reading next. Are you going to put in for the vicar's job?'

'I think not.'

'Why are we going to hospital, may I ask?'

'Young David Reed is back in the land of the living.'

Twenty minutes later they were standing by the hostel worker's bed. His partial recovery had provided exactly the break which Blizzard and his team needed, confronted as the police had been by twenty-four hours of headlines and media broadcasts focusing on the investigation into the shooting at The Spur. The force needed some good news because, as luck would have it, the dead boy was doubly newsworthy. Named the night before as 21-year-old Mark Ramford, a well-known drug addict, he had a 'hang-them-and-flog-them' magistrate for a father, a dyed-in-the-wool high-ranking local Conservative and a former mayor to boot. Blizzard quite liked him: his tough views on law and order had always chimed with those of the chief inspector whenever they shared public platforms.

The media were having another field day,

seizing with glee on the story on a quiet news weekend. It had not taken them long to unearth young Ramford's history. Having been a rebellious teenager, he had left home and only returned to beg for cash from his unsympathetic father. When that failed, he broke in and took the money instead. That was his first court appearance, followed by a string of others for theft, criminal damage and drug possession and a short prison sentence. On his release, the family had eventually lost touch with him until he had reappeared on The Spur, where he had been squatting and dealing drugs to feed his own habit. Off his head on a cocktail of heroin, cocaine and some white pills which he bought even though he didn't know what they were, Mark had panicked when he heard shouting on the landing and had burst out of the flat, brandishing what turned out to be a replica firearm. Now, he was lying on a mortuary slab and the Press were on the scent of the story.

Blizzard, although irritated that the force had been forced to defend itself over what he viewed as a justified act of self-defence by an officer with a gun pointed at him, was pleased about one thing, that the media had, for the moment, forgotten about his murder investigation. Blizzard was happiest when operating quietly away from the spotlight. If the media was looking elsewhere, Blizzard and his team could get on with their job without having to worry too much about the fall-out. And since leaving the police station the afternoon before, Blizzard had been doing a lot of thinking, as he explained to his sergeant as he manoeuvred his grimy Granada out into the light morning traffic. The interview with Henry Sanders had crystallized his thinking tremendously. It had been, he had told the sergeant, as if the fog had cleared as he sat on his sofa the previous night, reading and intermittently breaking off to stare into space and absent-mindedly swig his glass of whisky. It seemed certain, he said, that although Steve Holdsworth and the Reverend Henry Sanders were indeed inextricably linked, it was not by murder. That Josh Holdsworth had been killed was more of a tragic coincidence, the chief inspector had reasoned, rather than a consequence of the affair between his mother and the vicar.

Steve Holdsworth, Blizzard said, was simply a feckless man, prepared to lie about his own affair but unable to countenance his wife's dalliance with the vicar and prepared to mete out his own crude form of justice on the hapless clergyman. His lack of sensitivity about his son's death was the sign of a selfish and cruel man but not of a killer, Blizzard informed the nodding sergeant as they pulled into the hospital car-park. Colley had come to the same conclusion the night before. Indeed, Jay had told him off for drifting into similar reveries when they went out for a curry. The sergeant had heeded the warning: she was a mightily tolerant woman who rarely complained about his dedication to the job so when she complained, there was usually a good reason.

With Holdsworth and Sanders ruled out of the frame for the murders, that only seemed to leave Bob Maddox, Blizzard told Colley, as they walked across the car park. The chief inspector believed Maddox had found himself caught up in the events of the last few days because he was a man of low intelligence whose emotions and actions could easily be shaped by those shrewder than himself, Blizzard explained. There was no doubting his enduring and genuine sadness at the loss of his son two decades ago and Margaret Hatton, in her self-serving way, had recognized that, seizing on the opportunity to make it the fulcrum of her highly public protest against the church and its hostel, knowing that evoking the memory of Danny Maddox would make for good copy. Mix in to that, said Blizzard, the coincidental revelation that his good friend's wife was having an affair with the vicar and it all added up to a powerful cocktail of emotions targeted at the church. While he could not see Maddox killing Josh Holdsworth, Blizzard was pretty certain he had attacked David Reed and Glenda Rutherford.

Motive? asked Colley. Easy, said Blizzard

confidently. Maddox attacked David Reed because he saw him as a symbol of the hostel harbouring his son's murderer. Blizzard sketched out a scenario in which Maddox arrived in search of Albert Macklin, believing him still to be there despite police claims that the old man had left the city. Turning up just after Henry Sanders left the office that night— they probably never saw each other—Maddox had taken out his frustration on David Reed, possibly meaning only to hurt him rather than commit murder. Maddox had then killed Glenda Rutherford, said Blizzard, as they walked up the stairs to the ward, because he feared she had seen him leave the hostel. But, said Colley, she never mentioned him. Ah, said Blizzard, but Maddox did not know that. Rebuking himself for allowing himself to concentrate too heavily on the vicar, Blizzard entered the ward and told Colley that arresting Bob Maddox was now the top priority.

Lying in a side room, David Reed was a shadow of the young man they had seen at the hostel a week ago when the protests were under way. Face bloodless, lips almost blue, head swathed in bandages, he had lost a lot of weight and was lying propped up on pillows, hardly able to support himself. As they entered he turned sunken eyes towards them.

'David,' said Blizzard, sitting down on the chair next to the bed. 'How are you?'

'Not too great,' croaked the young man.

'You had us worried for a moment there.'

Reed closed his eyes and nodded feebly.

'Are you able to talk?' asked the chief inspector. The eyes opened again.

'I'll try.'

'We know you confronted Henry Sanders about the money. We think you gave him the chance to put it back. Are we right?'

A small nod of the head but no words. It was as if even nodding was too much of an effort.

'We think the vicar left the church shortly afterwards and that someone else attacked you. Was it Bob Maddox, by any chance?'

A firm shake of the head.

'Are you sure?'

'Yes.'

'How do you know? Was he there?'

'No.'

'Sure?'

'I'm not sure about anything.'

'Do you know who attacked you?'

There was silence as David Reed considered the question.

'David?'

'I'm trying to remember,' he explained at last, and shook his head in frustration, wincing at the pain, 'but I can't. I'm sorry.'

'What do you remember?' asked Colley.

'After Henry left,' and his brow was furrowed as he tried to recall, 'I started to do some paperwork. Then . . . no, nothing after that. I'm sorry.'

David Reed closed his eyes and the nurse who had been standing quietly at the door walked up the bed and looked at the chief inspector.

'That's all for now,' she said firmly. 'He needs rest.'

Blizzard nodded and he and the sergeant started to leave. As they reached the door, David Reed opened his eyes.

'Chief Inspector?' he said weakly.

Blizzard turned.

'Why would you think Bob Maddox attacked me?'

'I didn't say he did,' said Blizzard guardedly.

'But clearly you think it is possible.' Reed managed to sit up, helped by the nurse. 'So, why would he do that?'

'You were looking after Albert Macklin,' replied Blizzard. 'There was a lot of anger about. People weren't thinking straight.'

'But can they not find it in themselves to forgive?' said Reed sadly. 'If only they would let the Lord touch their hearts.'

Blizzard made no reply and walked out into the ward.

'Jesus,' he said outside. 'Do these people never learn?'

'It's their faith,' said Colley. 'They believe in forgiveness.'

'If you ask me,' retorted Blizzard setting off down the ward. 'Whoever whacked him didn't do it hard enough . . . maybe it would have knocked some sense into his stupid head.'

Colley followed him, grinning. 'They're going to love you in church,' he chuckled. 'They really are . . .'

CHAPTER TWENTY-SEVEN

They didn't love him in church. It might have been his distinctly secular approach to life that annoyed them, it might have been his perpetually brusque nature, but it was probably more likely the presence of a vanload of uniformed police officers sitting outside St Mary's as the faithful filed out of the Sunday morning service. Parked around neighbouring streets were other police vehicles, a number of them unmarked, one of which contained David Colley. Blizzard stood at the front gate of the church, watching the congregation leave, ignoring the hostile stares as he scanned the faces intently. After a few minutes, Edgar Rose-Harvey strode purposefully from the church, a thunderous expression on his face.

'Mr Blizzard,' he said angrily, 'I demand an explanation.'

'I think I might have mentioned before,' replied Blizzard coolly, 'that when I am running murder inquiries I do the demanding.'

Rose-Harvey glared at him, hesitated for a

moment then appeared to think twice about escalating the confrontation.

'In which case,' he said icily, bringing his emotions under control, 'I request to know why you are here.'

'Because of him,' said Blizzard, pointing to Bob Maddox as his quarry ambled out of the church, dressed incongruously in an ill-fitting dark suit, his peroxide blonde wife tottering alongside on her scarlet heels.

Maddox caught sight of the chief inspector, his eyes widened and he spun on his heels only to be confronted by a couple of plain-clothed detectives who had attended the service under cover. Maddox seemed to consider making a run for it but thought better of it and shrugged his shoulders. One of the officers cuffed his hands behind his back, watched by Maddox's horrified wife.

'How did you know I would be here?' he asked, as Blizzard approached.

'You might be a toerag,' replied the chief inspector, 'but you do have a heart—unlike your odious friend Steve. They tell me that every Sunday you light a candle for Danny.'

Tears welled in Maddox's eyes. Blizzard watched for a moment, fascinated yet again by the contrasting mixture of the hard, violent man and the loving father who had never come to terms with the loss of his teenaged son.

'I was pretty sure that you wouldn't miss,' said Blizzard.

'Never do,' mumbled Maddox.

'Take him away,' said Blizzard, nodding to the two plainclothed officers.

'Whereya takin' him?' asked Maddox's wife in her flat Hafton accent.

'Confession,' replied Blizzard drily.

Edgar Rose-Harvey watched Maddox bundled into the police van then turned to the chief inspector.

'I take it,' he said coldly, 'that this is the last of your antics at this church? I really would like us to return to normal life again.'

'I appreciate that,' said the chief inspector, 'but there are too many unanswered questions at the moment. Frankly, Mr Rose-Harvey, I would happily see your church closed down given what I have seen over the past week or so.'

'I do hope you do not mean that, Chief Inspector,' said Rose-Harvey archly. 'We have worked too hard to bring the light of the Lord into this church to give up now because of a few setbacks.'

'Setbacks! I hardly call two murders and a serious assault a setback!' exclaimed Blizzard. 'I call that bloody evil!'

'We are all sinners,' replied Rose-Harvey and his face assumed that faraway expression again. 'What Jesus Christ offers us is the chance of salvation.'

'You people,' groaned Blizzard.

'If only you would open your heart, Chief

Inspector,' replied Rose-Harvey sadly. 'The Lord offers us forgiveness. Turning His will into reality on Earth is our vision . . .'

'Double bloody vision more like,' snorted Blizzard, turning on his heel and stalking off down the path towards Colley, who had just ambled into view.

'You got him then?' asked the sergeant, as Maddox was bundled into the police van.

'Yes, no trouble.'

'And what about our friend Mr Rose-Harvey?'

'Started to deliver the sermon on the mount.'

'There's a surprise.'

'Indeed.' Blizzard walked round and climbed into the passenger seat of Colley's car. 'Come on, I suddenly feel a desperate desire for a bacon butty.'

CHAPTER TWENTY-EIGHT

It was early afternoon and, after a snatched lunch in the Abbey Road Police Station canteen, Blizzard and Colley were interviewing Bob Maddox. The big man's usual cant and bluster had been dissipated by the detectives' remorseless questioning for the best part of an hour. Often, interviewing teams played the classic 'nice cop, nasty cop' routine. Blizzard and Colley did it differently, both able to switch effortlessly between the two approaches as circumstances required. Maddox's initially confrontational approach made it pretty obvious to both of them that a tough line was required and they had fired questions at him like bullets from a machine-gun, their suspect bewildered by the speed at which they came, and the way the officers switched direction, one taking the lead then the other taking it back again.

His solicitor, the paunchy balding Eric Liddle, had said little during the interview. It was a style which made him respected among police officers in the city, not because it meant they had an easier task but because he was not preoccupied, like too many of his colleagues, with trying to trip up the interviewers and score points on behalf of their clients. Eric Liddle took the view that everyone wanted the same thing at the end of the day, the guilty people charged and the innocent people allowed to walk free. If he could make that process easier, he was happy.

Many words could have been used to describe Bob Maddox by 2.30 but happy was not one of them. He shifted uneasily in his seat as Blizzard and Colley stared wordlessly without emotion across the table at him during a pause in the questioning. For an hour, Maddox had fabricated a tissue of lies, concocting alibis about where he was on the nights of the attack on David Reed and the murder of Glenda Rutherford. Colley had slipped out briefly to have one of the inquiry team check them out and the detectives were pretty sure they were bogus, particularly given that they were corroborated by a veritable rogues' gallery. Maddox knew they did not believe him but had been reassured by the fact that the line of questioning seemed to suggest that the detectives had little hard evidence, relying instead on what sounded to him like guesswork. For their part, Blizzard and Colley were happy to let him lie his head off; Blizzard often called it giving them a spade and letting them dig. And Bob Maddox was digging so furiously they could virtually see the soil fly.

'Look,' said the chief inspector eventually, rapidly tiring of the game, 'this is getting us nowhere, Bob. We know you attacked David Reed and murdered Glenda Rutherford. Our forensics team have been going through your wardrobe . . .'

Eric Liddle sat forward and raised a quizzical eyebrow.

'Yes, we have a warrant,' said Blizzard.

Liddle nodded and sat back.

'Why are they doing that?' asked Maddox, perturbed at this revelation.

'There's always a fibre or something, you know,' said the chief inspector casually. 'Criminals always leave something of themselves behind.'

For the first time, Bob Maddox's bullish façade seemed shaken—but he covered it well, outwardly appearing to regain his composure even if his troubled eyes belied his anxiety.

'You're fishing,' he taunted them.

'It would be more fun that this,' said Blizzard, recalling contented summer childhood days on the river-banks on rural Lincolnshire, trying to catch chubb and bream with his father.

With a great effort he dragged himself back into the present day. Placing his hands behind his head, he rocked backwards on his chair and prepared to release his bombshell, which he did eventually by saying casually, 'Oh, by the way, David Reed has been very helpful.'

Maddox's mouth gaped open. For a few seconds he was too shocked to speak. As far as the city was concerned, David Reed was still in a coma, hovering between life and death. No one knew that he had regained consciousness and had spoken to the detectives that morning. And they definitely didn't know that, as Bob Maddox was being placed in a cell at Abbey Road Police Station that morning, Reed had asked a nurse to contact Blizzard again, her call interrupting the officers' lunch. Ramming the last of his bacon butty into his mouth, Blizzard had taken a last regretful gulp of tea and led the way out of the police station canteen.

What David Reed said over the next few

minutes behind the closed door in the hospital room had transformed and invigorated the investigation. Partly due to a partial return of his memory, partly a desire to unburden himself of what he knew, however painful it might be, he might not have solved the mystery but it had taken the detectives along a whole new line of inquiry which promised much and confirmed other evidence which the team had gathered painstakingly. Nevertheless, the claims he had made were so staggering, the revelations so dark, that Blizzard had sought the consultant's opinion that the young man was not suffering from some form of brain damage. Reassured that he was not, the chief inspector immediately ordered that David Reed's room be placed under round-the-clock police guard. For now, though, the chief inspector surveyed the uncomfortable Bob Maddox, the detective's mind finally made up about how to play one of his new trump cards.

Maddox, knowing none of this, blurted out, 'You're bluffing!'

'You wish.'

Maddox searched the chief inspector's eyes for a sign that he was making it up but found none, only blue ice. Maddox thought for a moment, his composure well and truly rattled.

'I aint saying nothing more,' he announced at length.

'You don't need to,' said Blizzard disarmingly. 'I'm sick of your lies anyway. We already know that you did it. According to David Reed, he remembers seeing you outside the church just before he was attacked. That places you at the scene, Bob.'

'I was . . . I . . . er . . . I goes to church some nights to pray for Danny,' blathered Maddox, gaining confidence in his own story. 'Yeah, that's it, Mr Blizzard, that's what happened. I went to the church that night to pray for Danny. I loved that boy.'

'I am sure you did. Tell me, how did you get into the church?'

It seemed an innocent enough question and Maddox fell right into the trap.

'The caretaker let me in.'

'Well, that's funny,' replied Blizzard with a hard edge to his voice, 'because we reckoned you might say that so we checked with him. He didn't let anyone in. In fact, he remembers the night well, not just because of what happened to David Reed but because it was his thirtieth wedding anniversary. He was even able to tell the sergeant here what he had for his meal down the Spice Gate Indian restaurant. A very pleasant rogan josh, was it not, Sergeant?'

'Apparently so,' nodded Colley. 'Quite spicy, he said.'

'You know,' smiled Blizzard, licking his lips, 'I could almost eat it myself right now. What about you, Bob?'

Maddox's eyes had widened and his mouth was opening and closing like the proverbial goldfish.

Blizzard eyed the yellowed teeth with distaste; why didn't people take more care of them? he mused idly as Maddox tried to regain his senses.

'I must have remembered it wrong. Perhaps it was someone else,' blustered the prisoner.

'Nice try, Bob, but your target was the hostel anyway—and that door was open apparently. David Reed reckons Glenda left it unlocked by accident when she went to the shops.'

It was an unequal struggle to which Maddox finally surrendered. The end when it came was so swift it surprised the detectives, who had expected a little more bluster from him.

'OK,' he whispered, sinking into his chair. 'OK.'

'That's more like it,' said Blizzard cheerfully then adding, that edge back into his voice, 'But, Bob, I don't want any heroics, right? No protecting anyone else. I want everything there is to know.'

'Don't worry.' Maddox leant forward, fire in his eyes and as he wagged a finger at the detectives. 'If I go down, I ain't going alone: you can be sure of that!'

CHAPTER TWENTY-NINE

'Did Tulley get the stuff?' asked Blizzard, rocking back on the chair in his office.

'On your desk,' said Colley, nodding towards a file on top of the largest pile of documents.

'Does it check out?' asked Ronald, who had gratefully given up a Sunday afternoon DIY shopping with his wife to watch the events unfolding.

'Certainly does. Tulley put a call into a mate of his in CID down there. Turns out they have had their suspicions for a while.'

'So why didn't they do anything about it?' asked Ronald.

'The CPS threw the file back. Said they did not have enough evidence to guarantee a conviction.'

'But surely it was worth a try?' said Ronald.

'CPS refused and that was that,' shrugged Colley.

'So it never became public?' asked Blizzard, passing the file to the superintendent.

'One of the woodentops ordered them not to,' explained the sergeant then clapped a hand to his mouth when Ronald glared at him. 'Oops, sorry, guv.'

'I should think you are,' said Ronald archly. 'As a woodentop myself, I would rather that you didn't use that phrase.'

'I said I was sorry,' grinned Colley.

Ronald humphed then read the file with mounting interest and not a little chagrin.

'They should have risked it,' he said with a shake of the head. 'A jury might have gone for it.'

'CPS reckoned it wouldn't even make trial,' explained Colley.

'You'd have thought they might have tipped off the press,' mused Blizzard. 'Would have saved an awful lot of trouble.'

'They thought about that,' nodded Colley. 'But everyone would have known where it came from. Remember, that was where that sergeant was sacked last year for leaking a story about the closing of the canteen at his station.'

'We had better be right about this,' said Ronald cautiously, looking at his chief inspector pointedly. 'The fall-out if we cock this one would be unimaginable. It would be a PR disaster. There's a lot of public sympathy for her after what she has been through.'

'*Says* she has been through,' corrected Blizzard.

'I am just saying you had better be right.'

'We're right,' said Blizzard confidently.

'I do hope so because if you're wrong we'll spend the rest of our days changing the film in speed cameras.'

'Don't worry,' said Blizzard, reassuringly,

'we're right, Arthur.'

'And if we're not,' interjected Colley brightly, 'I don't mind being the one that goes up the ladder.'

Blizzard roared with laughter. Ronald looked from the chief inspector to his sergeant and back again. Everything about their demeanour reassured him that they had got it right. He nodded.

'Bring her in,' he said.

It was late Sunday afternoon when the sleek white Jaguar was stopped by the patrol car on the motorway heading out of Hafton. Suspecting nothing, assuming she had been speeding, Margaret Hatton wound down her window and smiled at the traffic policeman but the smile froze as she saw in her wing mirror the approaching figures of John Blizzard and David Colley. One look at the stern expressions on their faces made her realize that the game was up.

Back in the interview room at Abbey Road Police Station, she looked at the detectives with a slight, but growing, sense of unease. Her last successful brush with the law had given her immense confidence, and the faces on those other detectives when they told her there would be no prosecution, had sustained her for a long time. But these two, she feared, were a tougher proposition; the other detectives seemed prepared to admit defeat, if only reluctantly. The steely look in Blizzard's eyes suggested that he and Colley were of a different mindset, that they were not prepared to let the matter of her criminal activities rest. After a whispered conversation with her lawyer, a weasely character called Edwards with whom Blizzard had clashed many a sword in the past, she sat up straight, composed, cool, confident. She had beaten off the police once, she would do it again.

'You've led us a right dance, Margaret,' began Blizzard, holding up the file. 'We didn't know your little secret until now.'

She eyed the file coolly, playing dumb.

'What secret, pray?'

'Well, where do we start?' said Blizzard, flicking through the file. 'How about the fact that your son was not murdered by a paedophile?'

She smiled calmly, she had gone through all this before.

'Not exactly.'

Cool, thought Colley.

'Not at all,' said Blizzard, steel in his voice. 'In fact, he lives in New Zealand.'

'Some might say it is just as bad,' replied Margaret Hatton, with a smile which masked her shock at the revelation that they knew where Kevin was.

The other officers had also guessed her paedophile story was fake but had not managed to track down her son, who had left the UK to escape the attentions of his conwoman mother. Since he had made his new start, he had not spoken to her and, keen to conceal his antecedents, he had never spoken about her to anyone, as far as she knew. As a result, many of her scams over the years had never been properly investigated. Blizzard noticed her confusion with satisfaction.

'Emigrated four years ago. Married with two kids. He disowned you, didn't he?'

She nodded, struck dumb.

'Changed his name. But we found him. One of my men talked to him yesterday. Nice lad. Detests you.'

'But how did you find him?' she asked hoarsely.

'Wonderful thing the Internet,' beamed Blizzard.

Advantage Blizzard, thought Colley. Margaret Hatton's head was bowed, and the voice was so quiet they could hardly make out the words.

'OK, I admit, I made the story up,' she said.

'So all of this protesting is just a charade?'

'No,' she spat back, suddenly reinvigorated, 'I believe in what I am doing! These paedophiles have to be—'

'Cut the crap!' snorted Blizzard. 'This is all about getting your face in the media!'

'No, it's not, I truly—'

'In fact, based on your pack of lies, you have received more than eighty thousand pounds in charitable and government grants and a number of councils have hired you as a consultant on child protection issues at, no doubt, a very healthy fee.'

'Yes, they have but—'

'Including our good Councillor Gallagher. I believe he hired you to take a series of workshops in the city next spring after meeting you at your protest outside City Hall. I can't wait to see his face when I tell him.'

'I shouldn't get too smug,' said Margaret Hatton, regaining her poise. 'What do you think a court will say to this? Yes, I committed fraud—but only to protect the children. It's all for the children, Chief Inspector. Even if a jury does find me guilty—and how many of them will have children, do you think?—the most the judge will give me is a suspended sentence. You might have your day in court, Chief Inspector, but mine will be the victory.'

'You may be right,' said Blizzard calmly, putting down the file. 'But then we don't want to question you about the fraud.'

Her expression said it all: alarm, consternation, fear. Blizzard did not allow his feelings to show but inside, he was cheering. In front of him, Margaret Hatton's composure had been shattered, just like it had been with Bob Maddox. The upper hand was his now, and anyone who had played poker with Blizzard knew that when he had the right cards, there was no one who could defeat him.

'No,' he said casually, 'we want to talk to

226

you about the attack on David Reed and the murder of Glenda Rutherford.'

She tried to regain her composure but found it impossible.

'What do you mean?' she whispered.

'Bob Maddox has such a sweet singing voice,' said Blizzard. 'He told us how you convinced him that the only way to get even for his son's death was to attack the hostel. Pretty easy, I should think—he's been angry for nearly twenty years.'

'He's making it up.'

'I don't think so. He says you suggested he attack someone there as a warning, to frighten them. But he went too far, almost killed young David Reed.'

'He's a damned fool!' rasped Margaret. 'A damned fool! He was only supposed to h—'

She clapped her hand to her mouth as she realized the enormity of her words but it was too late.

'I am sure the tape caught that,' smiled Blizzard, thinly. 'What do you think the jury would say now?'

'Tell us about Glenda Rutherford,' said Colley, keeping up the pressure. 'Why did she have to die?'

She sighed. 'Bob didn't realize she was on duty that night—she'd gone out to the shops or something. When he found out she was there, he couldn't take the risk that she had seen him. It was Bob's idea to kill her.'

'I just hope it was all worth it, Margaret,' said Blizzard with a shake of the head.

'It would have been. I had just applied for a large charitable grant and I needed something to get me back into the headlines, to make everyone realize how important we are. The death of Josh Holdsworth has been ideal—'

'Not exactly the phrase I would have used,' said Blizzard sharply, adding pointedly, 'Particularly not for someone who "does it for the children".'

She realized the insensitivity of her comments and quickly corrected herself.

'Of course, it was tragic. Absolutely tragic. What I meant was that the hostel was ideal for our needs and Albert Macklin was Heaven sent.'

'Another poor choice of words,' murmured Blizzard.

'Perhaps—but the plan would have worked. People were already worried about the hostel, the death of poor Josh made them feel frightened, public opinion would have built, the hostel staff would have been terrified by the attack, the church would have closed the place and all the credit would have gone to us. The grant would have been in the bag.'

She looked at them sadly.

'But Bob Maddox mucked it all up.'

Blizzard sighed. 'I'm sure Glenda Rutherford's husband agrees,' he said.

'Like I said,' and the voice was cool and

collected again as she glanced at the tape machine, already laying the groundwork for her defence in court, 'it was all a terrible mistake. I never meant for David Reed to be so badly injured and Bob decided to kill Glenda himself. I entreated him not to but he wouldn't listen. I am sure a jury would believe me.'

She smiled sweetly. How could a jury resist that smile? Blizzard gave a contemptuous snort then changed tack.

'And what about Josh Holdsworth? How do I know that you didn't order Bob to kill him as well?'

'No!'

The voice was full of anger at the suggestion. Genuine emotion this time. She glared at him.

'No, never! Whatever you think of me, I have the best interests of the children at heart. Always, Chief Inspector, always!'

'Now why do I find that difficult to believe?' murmured Blizzard, switching off the tape, pushing back his chair and heading for the door, followed by Colley.

'We will continue this conversation later,' he said.

Outside in the corridor, Blizzard stood with his back resting against the wall and closed his eyes.

'So what do you think?' said Colley.

'She's a cool customer, I'll give her that.

With what we have at the moment, a jury might do her for conspiracy but she could probably convince them that it was all down to Bob.'

'And Josh?'

'No'

'Sure?'

'Sure.'

Colley's mobile phone went off. He listened intently for a few moments then replaced it in his pocket.

'Tulley,' he said.

'And?'

'Chummy has turned up. They're bringing him in.'

Half an hour later, Tulley was back at the station with James Calvert, the businessman, dressed in a sharp dark suit even though it was Sunday. He seemed nervous, with none of the confident front which had characterized the sergeant's last meeting with him. His eyes darted about anxiously as he was led into the interview-room, as if he expected someone to leap out and attack him. Blizzard and Colley sat down opposite him and watched him with interest, waiting for him to speak.

At length, he looked up. 'You know then?'

The detectives nodded. Twenty-five minutes later, it was all over, the story having tumbled out from the businessman's lips in a rush. He had been keen to unburden himself of his secret, had been toying with the idea of coming in to volunteer the information himself. After he had agreed to give a statement, the detectives headed back out into the corridor.

'Yes,' whispered Blizzard, punching the air. 'Yes bloody yes!'

Colley grinned. 'That confirms it,' he said. 'Just shows, like you always say, if you shake enough trees there's no knowing what will fall out. So what do you think? Do you reckon our man will try something else tonight?'

'Got to be a good chance. We'd better get something planned. Be nice to catch him in the act.'

'I'll round up some troops.'

'Thanks,' replied Blizzard, as his sergeant headed briskly down the corridor. 'Oh, David?'

Colley turned round.

'I don't want anyone outside this station finding out that we have Margaret Hatton or James Calvert here. If word gets out it could wreck everything . . . and that, as Arthur is fond of saying, would indeed be a PR disaster.'

CHAPTER THIRTY

'Another late night with you,' sighed Blizzard as they sat in the car, 'people will be thinking we are an item.'

'You don't have the legs for it,' chuckled Colley. Blizzard considered the thought of Jay in a skirt and nodded in the darkness.

'I can see your good lady has certain charms which I don't.'

'I hope you've not been ogling my girlfriend,' remarked Colley. 'Besides, given your love of trains—'

'Locomotives,' corrected Blizzard. 'They're locomotives.'

'Whatever you call them, given your love of locomotives, wouldn't you be happier with someone covered in oil and wearing a boiler suit?'

'You can never know,' said Blizzard, 'the image that conjures up.'

Another chuckle through the darkness from the sergeant.

'You've been on your own too long,' he said.

It was just before midnight on the cloudy, overcast Sunday night, and they were sitting in an unmarked police car which had been parked in the shadows near St Mary's Church. Blizzard had left his Granada at Abbey Road to avoid anyone recognizing it. At the other end of the street was another vehicle containing DI Ramsey and Tulley, and stationed in surrounding streets were other vehicles, all unmarked, all crewed by officers in plainclothes. Secrecy being the key to the success of the operation, the cars had all been parked in the darkest corners of the streets and, in two cases, street lights had even been disabled earlier in the day by officers posing as council workmen. To further increase the chances of success, Blizzard had stressed that not a uniform must be seen in the area that night, that routine inquiries had to be suspended and mobile units keep away.

Things had moved quickly that afternoon following the interview with a guilt-ridden and frightened James Calvert, who had become increasingly alarmed at the depths of the waters in which he had chosen to swim and seemed relieved when the detectives brought him in for questioning. To confirm his story, which tallied with the one recounted earlier in the day by David Reed, detectives had been busy wrecking Sunday afternoons, visiting council officers at their homes, Blizzard briefing the bishop at his official residence on the outskirts of the city and Ronald tracking down the chief constable at his golf club and appraising him of the situation. Involving chief constables in inquiries went against the grain with all of them and was a calculated risk because sometimes chiefs wanted to take personal command of situations. Everyone remembered how the last deputy chief damned near got himself shot when he wandered across the line of fire during an armed seige in one of the terraced streets. However, given the high profile nature of the inquiry there was no option and, thankfully, the chief constable placed his trust in the experienced detective chief superintendent. Ronald, for his part, had transferred that trust down the line to Blizzard, who had played a roving role throughout the afternoon and evening, constantly taking calls on his mobile as his detectives appraised him of the information which gradually allowed him to fit the last pieces of the jigsaw into place.

At six o'clock, he, Ronald, DI Ramsey, and Colley held a meeting in the superintendent's office over take-away pizza—everyone ignoring Blizzard's tutting as he poked it scornfully—and resolved their plan of action. Ronald was in overall command but decided to stay with one of the back-up units and let John Blizzard work, as usual, with Colley, and Ramsey and Tulley team up in the other frontline car, their good working relationship over several years guaranteeing excellent support.

Although the church was the object of their interest, the officers had deliberately kept away during the evening service; the last thing they wanted to do was risk a confrontation with the irate Edgar Rose-Harvey, who already regarded them as having overstepped the bounds and shown scant respect for the sanctity of the church. Indeed, there were rumours that he was planning to lodge a harassment complaint against John Blizzard. The chief inspector was not too worried—such moves, he reasoned, suggested he was doing his job properly—but he did not particularly relish the distractions it could cause. So, he gambled that beginning the operation after the evening service and the youth fellowship had finished was the right course of action. Nothing, he believed, was likely to happen for several hours anyway. If it happened at all.

Edgar Rose-Harvey had not been idle himself, going onto a local radio station's religious magazine programme that morning to accentuate his claims for the church as the victim. In strong language, he condemned those who said that St Mary's should close because of the damage done by the events of the past week and the fact that it had become such a magnet for protests and vandalism. He did not mention that Blizzard was one of those who had made such a suggestion but the meaning was clear enough to the chief inspector, listening with pursed lips to the interview in his office. The radio station had invited the police to respond but Ronald had declined to take part, on advice from the press office. It turned out to be a wise decision because it was an increasingly angry interview with Rose-Harvey dismissing all the show host's attempts to put the other side of the argument and maintaining that it was wrong to blacken the name of the church and its God-fearing congregation.

The church remained committed, said Edgar Rose-Harvey, to the idea of the hostel

235

and, whatever the strength of local protests, would continue to take in paedophiles if it felt that the power of the risen Lord could help make a change in their lives. If the church closed the hostel, he said passionately, it would undermine everything they had been trying to achieve at St Mary's. It would also, he argued, be a victory for violence and intimidation.

Following the interview, the radio station contacted Councillor Gallagher, who reiterated his support for the hostel. Yes, he had said equally passionately, there were risks involved in running such a place but sometimes those risks needed to be taken and he was prepared to support St Mary's all the way. His final comment was, Blizzard suspected, a thinly veiled rebuke aimed specifically at him, Gallagher saying that there were some people in the city who were living in the stone age and who needed to be brought into the modern world. This was 1993, he reminded the listeners. Blizzard had smiled thinly. Whatever he might have thought of the councillor, the chief inspector had to admit that he was an impressive and erudite speaker. Even if it was all cobblers.

So, the detectives had edged their cars into place shortly before 9.30, waiting for the last of the lights to go out in the church as the unsuspecting caretaker locked up and left for home. Next door, lights in the hostel also went out one by one, the only remaining illumination coming from the office where the night duty manager was stationed. Lights were being switched off in the terraced houses surrounding the church as well, residents climbing the stairs to bed. By midnight, the detectives had the streets to themselves, having watched glumly as the last of the drunks had reeled past their vehicles, wending their weary way home. Eventually, just before one o'clock, with Blizzard wondering whether or not to call off the operation and with the streets home only to the increasingly chilly detectives and the occasional cat skulking in the shadows, something happened. It was Colley who spotted it first, a movement in the darkest corner of the garden, almost parallel with their car. The detectives sank deeper into their seats and peered into the night as best they could from their low vantage point. There was definitely someone picking their way between the apple trees. Two people, in fact, both dressed in dark clothes and with their faces partially obscured by balaclavas. One of them appeared to have a bulky haversack on his back. They spent several seconds looking hard at the car but concluded that it was empty, unable to make out the detectives in the inky blackness.

Then they walked tentatively across the garden, away from the car and towards the church, constantly looking around to make sure that no one was watching. As they edged their way along the side of the church and slipped round to the front, standing beneath the large stained-glass window, they were partly illuminated by one of the street lights. They gave the street a final scan then each grabbed a drainpipe on either side of the stained glass window. The watching detectives could see some loose brickwork come away in the hands of one of the men.

'Recognize them?' whispered Blizzard.

'Difficult to see,' murmured Colley. 'But the guy with the bag looks very like the one I chased after Glenda Rutherford's murder.'

'Interesting,' breathed Blizzard then said quietly into his radio, 'Nobody moves. On my command only.'

Sitting at either end of the street, the four detectives watched in fascination as the men swiftly climbed the drainpipes.

'What do you think they are doing?' hissed Colley.

'Well, I don't think they're the window cleaners.'

A low chuckle from the sergeant.

Having clambered nimbly up the drainpipes, the men swung themselves over the guttering and onto the roof. The man lowered his haversack and together they bundled out a bulky object. As they unfurled it, it soon revealed itself as some kind of banner but the detectives could not make out the words from such distance and in such darkness. Standing

238

on the roof edge, the men held a hurried conversation then stretched out the banner. Quickly they started to tie the ends to the drainpipes and lowered the material over the top half of the window, obscuring Jesus Christ's face.

'Go, go, go!' exclaimed Blizzard into his radio.

He and the sergeant leapt from their cars and ran towards the church. Ramsey and Tulley did likewise from the other end, able to make out the words as they approached. NO MORE PERVERTS. The men on the roof heard them coming and glanced down in horror. One of them seemed rooted to the spot but the one with the bag swung himself recklessly over the edge and started to shin down the drainpipe, hands grasping frantically for secure holds.

'Stop, police!' shouted Blizzard.

But the man ignored the command and kept climbing. Halfway down, though, he caught his foot between pipe and wall and with a yell twisted outwards. Making a desperate grab for the drainpipe, he screamed as it came away in his hands. Desperately, he hurled himself towards the wall but missed and with a terrible shattering of glass and a terrified screech, he plunged through the window, into the darkness of the church. They heard a dull thud from inside—then silence.

'Bloody hell!' cried Blizzard, and leaving

Ramsey and Tulley to coax down the horrified accomplice, he and Colley rushed round to the front door.

Colley kicked it in savagely and, snapping on lights as they went, the detectives raced into the church and over to the window, coming to a halt and staring in horror at the sight which met their gaze. There, sprawled obscenely across the stage, limbs twisted beneath him, was the man, a huge shard of glass jutting out of his chest, stained glass but with blood, a pool of which was already slowly spreading across the floor. Approaching slowly, hardly daring to look, Blizzard reached down, his feet crunching on glass, and pulled aside the balaclava so they could identity him.

'Is it him?' asked Colley, ashen-faced.

'I am afraid so,' nodded Blizzard, shaking his head. Looking into the lifeless face of Edgar Rose-Harvey, he murmured. ' "Vengeance is mine, saith the Lord".'

'Is he dead?'

'Yes,' nodded the chief inspector, straightening up.

He looked up at the jagged edges of the gaping hole in the window.

'I never did like that picture,' he said quietly, before walking out of the church and into the night.

CHAPTER THIRTY-ONE

'He had us all fooled,' said Ronald, sitting back in the chair in his office on the Monday morning, and shaking his head with disbelief.

'It would appear so,' replied Blizzard, who was standing at the window and staring at the drizzle as he cradled his mug of tea. 'Maybe I should have seen it earlier.'

'You can't blame yourself,' said Colley, who was sitting at the desk.

'Maybe.'

'Come on, John,' remonstrated Ronald. 'He was very clever even for your brain and he did provide us with a lot of red herrings.'

'The loaf and the fishes really,' said Colley brightly, grinning as the others turned pained expressions in his direction.

'You don't get any better do you?' said the chief inspector.

'Sorry,' beamed Colley, taking a sip and grimacing. 'Bloody hell, your tea doesn't get any better either, guv!'

'It's that new temp,' nodded Ronald gloomily. 'I'm sure she spits in it.'

Blizzard and Colley pulled faces and hurriedly placed their mugs on the desk. They were taking a well-earned break from a frantic morning of inquiries. Events had moved quickly since Edgar Rose-Harvey plunged to his death through the church window the night before. The detectives had known much of the story before they organized the surveillance of St Mary's and searches of Rose-Harvey's pleasant semi-detached house on the edge of the city first thing that morning had confirmed the rest.

Colley had attended as the search team ripped the house apart and the incriminating documents were discovered concealed beneath floorboards in the back bedroom. They confirmed what Tulley had unearthed during his diligent inquiries over recent days and supported the testimony of David Reed and James Calvert. None of it made for pretty reading. For a start, it turned out the dead man was not Edgar Rose-Harvey at all but had fabricated a fake identity in order to wheedle his way into the congregation at the church. He was really called Matthew St Clair, a man who was used to moving in society's higher circles.

Born the son of a peer of the realm in Essex, he had grown up in the rarified atmosphere of a large stately home in the country, all gravel drives, sweeping drawing rooms, ornate sculptures and repressed emotions. Rebelling against his life of privilege, he went off the rails, moved to London as a student and soon found himself hooked on drink and drugs and unceremoniously thrown off his economics degree course for non-attendance and an unsavoury drunken incident with the 15-year-old daughter of a professor. He should have been charged with the molestation of the girl but the university was desperate to hush things up. Bad publicity did not do anyone any favours. Eventually, though, he was jailed for six months for a string of minor deceptions—minor, that is, when compared with what he tried to perpetrate against the trusting congregation of St Mary's five years later.

That prison sentence was, however, the end of Matthew St Clair. While Matthew St Clair might have gone into prison, he did not come out. It was a bewildering array of other people who walked out of the prison gates and, using their bogus names, he embarked on a series of sophisticated financial frauds in various parts of the country, always distancing themselves from the actual offence. Never caught, never suspected, always outwardly respectable, always preying on his victims' trusting nature, always on the move.

Then he hit on the idea to sell St Mary's Church to the property company seeking a site for its supermarket and became Edgar Rose-Harvey, born-again Christian but same old conman. Never a Christian—a reaction against too many of his father's overfed rector friends when he was a boy—Rose-Harvey had nevertheless been attracted to St Mary's because of the prime site on which it stood, just a short distance from the city centre. Having read in the *Financial Times* that a major supermarket plan for Hafton had collapsed—ironically, on the site where Blizzard and his friends worked on The Silver Flyer—he got to thinking how he could use the situation to his advantage.

It did not take him long to become accepted by an evangelical group in his own area and when he moved to Hafton shortly afterwards, claiming a work transfer, his plan was well under way. Pledging to revitalize St Mary's, he persuaded a number of his trusting acolytes, earnest young men and women, to come with him. Dazzled by the way he invoked the Lord in all that he did, they unquestioningly gave up their jobs and college studies and blithely followed him to the city. Blind faith, Blizzard had grunted as the story had unfolded, could get you a long way and such was the power of Rose-Harvey's magnetic personality, and apparent religious fervour, that in a short time he had gathered round him a remarkably loyal number of ardent Christians at St Mary's, not just his original followers but evangelicals from around the city and further afield, all inspired by the feeling that something special was happening. Soon everyone was talking about the transformation at St Mary's and how the light of the Lord truly shone on the faces of its parishioners. This was helped by visits from several high profile evangelical preachers from around the country, one of whom was a friend of Rose-Harvey, an out-of-work actor who once made a minor appearance in 'EastEnders', buying oranges at one of the market stalls.

Rose-Harvey, ever the pragmatist, did not rely on emotion alone, though, ensuring that the power of the Spirit was helped by the power of corrupted democracy, recruiting enough supporters to vote out the established, more traditional, hierarchy at St Mary's and installing himself as the leader instead. The result was that parishioners who might have made life difficult, mostly retired men and women who had attended the church for many years, drifted away, finding other churches or ending their worshipping days altogether, their protests drowned out by the sound of tambourines and guitars as Sunday services took on a livelier, more modern atmosphere.

It was a highly effective ploy when congregation numbers were up and the congregation plate was overflowing week in, week out. Once established at St Mary's, Rose-Harvey needed to make his plan come to fruition—and quickly lest anyone become suspicious of his true motives. Realizing that no one in the congregation would allow him to sell the site when the church was proving so successful, he put the second phase of his plan into action. The scheme was devastatingly simple, the best ones always were. That had always been his mantra. Devise a simple scheme then weave complex patterns of deceptions around it. Like a spider with a web. Which was why he had the idea of the hostel—just about the most unpopular thing he could ever have dreamed up.

Knowing that many people in the area still felt the loss of young Danny Maddox keenly, Edgar Rose-Harvey invoked the power of the Lord to enthuse his followers with a zeal to help reform criminals, his powerful oratory easily persuading the evangelical church members to follow him and vote through the scheme and sweep away protests from a few voices within the congregation. Those remaining die-hards who opposed the idea said their piece then quit in disgust. Rose-Harvey then earned the trust of Councillor Gallagher, exploiting his liberal beliefs with the suggestion that such an enlightened approach to prison reform would earn him great personal kudos. Rose-Harvey even raised the prospect of an OBE. People, he always felt, were like musical instruments; you just had to know which tune to play.

The rest was simple, and Rose-Harvey sat back and watched the unsuspecting flies wander into his web. There had been protests when the hostel opened but not enough for his needs so he drummed up more vigorous local opposition by making sure that Margaret Hatton knew what was happening. She was, predictably, outraged and when she heard that Albert Macklin was due to be housed in the hostel—arranged by Councillor Gallagher—her arrival in the city breathed new vigour into the protests. Once the protests made the future of the church untenable, all he had to do was persuade the congregation to sell it to the developer and build a bigger, better church elsewhere, get the official permissions through and cream off some of the money in the process.

'So are you going to wrap things up now?' asked Ronald, as he and Colley headed for the door.

'Yep,' nodded the chief inspector. 'And nothing will give me greater pleasure.'

Five minutes later they were sitting in the interview-room, staring across the desk at Margaret Hatton, who had spent her time in police custody regaining her composure. Convinced that no court in the land would send her to jail once she had told her lies from the witness box, she was ever more confident that she might even escape prosecution, leaving the luckless Bob Maddox to take the fall.

'I take it you have come to release me? Slap wrists and all that?' she asked coolly.

Noticing the grave expressions on the detectives' faces, the first signs of anxiety crossed her face.

'What's wrong?'

'I am afraid we have some bad news,' said Blizzard. 'Your boyfriend is dead.'

'But I don't have a boyf—'

The voice tailed off as she stared at them in horror. 'Oh, no, not Matt . . . Tell me, it's not Matt,' she whispered hoarsely.

' "The Lord giveth and the Lord taketh away",' nodded Blizzard. 'Died last night trying to hang a protest banner from the church roof. Part of your little plan, I believe.'

She sat sobbing quietly. Blizzard, satisfied that he had, at last, gained the upper hand over her, felt little compassion; Margaret Hatton had exploited too many trusting people for that. Besides, her sobbing sounded too contrived to be sincere. Blizzard had been sceptical of her motives from the outset and was always convinced that she was tied up with whatever was happening at St Mary's, even if he did not know how. Detectives had been delving deeper into her background, but it was only when the search of Edgar Rose-Harvey's house found documents connecting the two that they realized just how extensive her deception had been. Rose-Harvey's original idea had been to create enough protests to make the future of the church untenable but Margaret Hatton had her own, more radical agenda in which people were tools to be used if there was money at the end of the process. Rose-Harvey had been deeply impressed by her pragmatic approach, recognizing in her a fellow exploiter of the weak-minded. Such criminally brilliant minds should be able to work together for their mutual benefit, he reasoned. Having been contacted by Edgar Rose-Harvey and offered money to spark protests in Hafton, the couple had discovered themselves kindred spirits and quickly became lovers.

Now Margaret Hatton turned those dark eyes on Blizzard, tears drying within seconds.

'How long have you known about us?'

'Not long. It has certainly been—if you will pardon the expression—an unholy alliance.'

'It was a brilliant plan,' she sighed, shaking her head.

'What exactly was the plan?' asked Blizzard. 'And don't keep anything back, we know most of it anyway.'

'So I see,' she said and took a deep breath. 'The idea was to create so much panic that people would happily sell the church. If we made it bad enough, who could object? Besides, they would have done anything for a shiny new church. Even the humble are vain, Chief Inspector.'

'Then?'

'Matt found a way of intercepting some of the cash. After that, we were going to head off into the sunshine before anyone noticed.'

'And I take it you persuaded Bob Maddox to attack David Reed to make people even more frightened?'

'Yes. Matt wanted to stick to spraying graffiti on the church and hanging banners, but I said it needed more. Attacking David Reed was obvious . . . and Bob Maddox was only too keen to do it.'

'Then frame the vicar?'

She nodded.

'Positively framed himself. Matt had known for a while that he was stealing from the church but he kept quiet. Said it would come in useful. So he left a couple of documents lying around to make David realize what the vicar was doing then waited for him to confront Henry. Then he sent Bob in to attack him afterwards.'

'But try to fool us it was a rock thrown by a protestor?' asked Colley.

'Yes. He knew you'd work it out but he reckoned it might confuse you for a day or two. And he knew you'd clear Henry in the end but he said it would give us some more time.'

'And Glenda Rutherford?' asked Blizzard.

'She was not in the original plan, but once it became clear that she might have seen Bob leave the office, we had to kill her,' said Margaret Hatton in a matter-of-fact voice. 'In fact, it was Matt who opened the church door to let him in. It was Matt your poor sergeant chased.'

'We guessed that,' nodded Blizzard. 'Forensics reckon a black fibre from the back wall matched one on the jumper your boyfriend was wearing last night.'

Mention of the death silenced her for a moment then she started to giggle. They looked at her in amazement.

'Pray, what is so funny?' asked Blizzard archly.

'Edgar thought it was amusing that while your sergeant here was chasing him over the church wall, Bob was hiding behind the bins just a few yards away.'

'I'm glad you find it funny,' murmured Colley, instinctively holding his bandaged hand.

'I assume that in addition to the banner last night,' said Blizzard, 'Matt was the one who spray-painted the obscenities on the church and smashed those side windows last week?'

Yes,' she nodded. 'Said it kept the pressure on.'

'Kevin Hurley,' said Colley, thinking about the accomplice on the roof, an earnest young parishioner who had been coaxed down in a state of shock the night before, 'said he did it because your boyfriend told him the protests were the only way to get the funding for a new church.'

'And it was working, wasn't it?' said Margaret with satisfaction.

The detectives nodded; the congregation was already down a third on the previous week, people deterred by a mixture of fear and remorseless media attention, sick of having cameras focused on them whenever they arrived for services. Rose-Harvey knew that they would probably have come back eventually but he was not about to let that happen; he had planned to let things carry on for a week or two, then reluctantly announce that, tragic as it was, the church would have to close and the hostel with it.

He would, according to Calvert, announce that the London-based property developer who had hoped to provide a site for the supermarket elsewhere in the city, had approached him—when in fact it had been the other way round some weeks before—and that the proceeds from the sale would allow a new church to be built elsewhere, bigger, better, grander, a true testament to the Lord. Rose-Harvey knew he could make it all sound like the Good News. It certainly would have been for him.

'You might even have got away with it,' commented Blizzard.

'We might well have,' she nodded sadly. 'How did you find out what we were doing?'

'We knew a lot of it—David Reed had worked some of it out—but we were helped by a spot of good old-fashioned Christian guilt.'

'Come again?'

'James Calvert.'

Bank records had linked Calvert to Edgar Rose-Harvey, who had needed a commercial figure to help him make contact with the property company. Calvert had had dealings with them in the past and Rose-Harvey befriended the unwitting businessman and quickly gleaned from him that his company was in financial trouble. The rest was easy as Calvert was lured into the trap, driven by the desperate need to clear his debts, then finding himself in too deep when the true evil nature of the plan became clear. Rose-Harvey had gambled that Calvert would keep quiet for fear of prosecution but he had misjudged the businessman's sense of mounting horror at what was happening.

'I take it he spilled his guts?' asked Margaret, the ugly phrase somehow seeming incongruous from her refined lips.

'Only too happy to,' and Blizzard gave a thin smile. 'There is honour among thieves, after all.'

'I told Matt we should not have roped him into it. He was all right when he thought he would make a lot of money but when things got nasty . . .' Her voice tailed off and she shook her head. 'No backbone, some people.'

'Anything else to add?' asked Blizzard, hardly able to conceal his revulsion at the calculating way in which she and Edgar Rose-Harvey had cynically exploited people.

She thought for a moment.

'Aren't you going to ask me about Josh Holdsworth?'

'No need.'

She nodded. 'I think you know who did that already.'

Blizzard nodded. 'Always have,' he said.

'See, I was right,' she said.

'What you did can never be right.'

Margaret Hatton pulled herself up straight in her chair and said calmly, 'So what happens now, Mr Blizzard?'

'You and Bob Maddox will stand trial for the murder of Glenda Rutherford and the assault on David Reed—I may even push for attempted murder. Somehow,' and Blizzard pushed back his chair with a scraping sound and headed for the door, 'I don't think they'll let you off after all, do you?'

CHAPTER THIRTY-TWO

The call which led the detectives to the killer of Josh Holdsworth came on the Tuesday morning—and it came from Colley's contact Chaz. In return for help seeking drug rehabilitation, Chaz had agreed to the sergeant's suggestion that he let himself be booked into the St Mary's hostel, something which Arthur Ronald managed to arrange by calling in a few favours. Chaz had spent a couple of days there and befriended one of the other residents, who quickly let slip in an unguarded moment the address which the detectives had been searching for.

Blizzard's original hunch that their man was not far away—and never had been—had proved true and now he and Colley were standing outside a run-down Victorian terraced house in Albert Street, half a mile from St Mary's Church. Days of Victorian grandeur long behind it, the street was sad and neglected. Indeed, there was talk among councillors of demolishing the houses altogether and redeveloping the site. There was a certain irony to that, thought Blizzard, given the events at the church over the past few days.

Now, having eased his way past the gate hanging off its hinges, he knocked loudly on the front door twice but there was no answer. Colley peered through the grubby window.

'Can't see much,' he said. 'It looks empty.'

'OK,' nodded Blizzard. 'After you, dear boy.'

The sergeant shoulder-charged the front door in best rugby style and it gave way with a tearing of hinges and cracking of wood. The officers stepped into the long, dark hall and recoiled as the stench hit them immediately. They knew immediately what it was—death always smelled the same. As their eyes became accustomed to the gloom, they edged their way down the hall towards the source of the smell, fearful of what they might find, but already knowing what it was. Pushing their way tentatively into the back room, they stood and stared at the body lying on the filthy sofa pushed up against the wall, the only piece of furniture on the bare boards. The corpse had clearly been there several days and the body had started to decompose, although to their relief the process had been slowed down by the chill air of the house. It was still recognizable, though.

'Albert Macklin,' said Colley, wrinkling his nose and peering into the bloated face with its lifeless eyes. 'No doubt about it.'

'Never was,' replied Blizzard.

Colley whipped out his handkerchief and gingerly held up an empty tablet bottle, which was lying next to an empty bottle of whisky.

'Suicide?' he asked, looking at his chief inspector.

'Kill or cure,' nodded Blizzard, 'Without the cure. Paedophiles never change. Oddly enough, Margaret Hatton was right about that—and I think Albert Macklin knew it. Hello, what's this?'

He walked over to the mantelpiece and picked up a small white envelope propped up against a dusty clock which had long since given up telling the time. Noticing his name scrawled on the front in untidy crabby hand-writing, Blizzard opened the envelope and slowly pulled out a single sheet of writing paper.

'A message from beyond the grave,' he said

dispassionately and began to read aloud, watched intently by the sergeant.

Dear Mr Blizzard, it said, and the chief inspector could hear Albert Macklin's nasal voice as he read, *By the time you read this I will be long dead. As you will have guessed by now, I killed Josh Holdsworth. It was an accident, not that I expect you to believe that.*

'In a funny way I do,' murmured Blizzard.

I really did mean to change this time and I really did mean to leave the city. I even packed my bags and left the hostel but I went down to the canal one last time before I went—hoped it would lay some ghosts, I suppose. And there he was. The old urges came back. They always do. He struggled to get away and I hit him. Why, you may ask, did I have a baseball bat with me?

'The thought had occurred,' grunted Blizzard.

The answer is simple. People were out to get me and I felt I needed something to defend myself with. The store-room in the church was open so I took the bat. I didn't mean to use it on the poor boy but he just kept struggling. I didn't mean to kill him. Please tell his parents I am sorry about that. Really sorry.

'More sorry than his dad,' commented Colley, darkly.

'Indeed,' nodded Blizzard and read on: *I couldn't do time again so this was the only way out, Mr Blizzard. Maybe I will bump into Dennis Barry in the after-life.*

'Dennis would love that,' muttered Blizzard and read the final passage. *I don't expect you to believe, or understand, what I say—nobody ever does. Oh, and before you ask, I did this terrible thing alone. Guess I will have to take the rest of my secrets to my grave. Sorry about that.*

Blizzard lowered the piece of paper for a moment; he felt he could almost hear the old man's low laugh as he deprived Blizzard of his best opportunity yet of breaking into the sex ring. The chief inspector returned his gaze to the letter.

Got to go now, he read, *Feeling woozy. God bless, Mr Blizzard.*

'I do wish,' said Blizzard, putting the letter into his pocket and heading out down the hall, 'that people would stop mentioning Him. He's caused quite enough trouble as it is.'

And, followed by his sergeant, he walked from the gloom of the house out into the bright sunshine and welcome fresh air of a Hafton winter morning.

EPILOGUE

'So it's all down to old-fashioned greed?' said an acutely disappointed Max Randall with a shake of the head as Blizzard and Colley finished their account.

It was the Thursday night and the three of them had joined Arthur Ronald and Alex Mather in a small pub in a village just the other side of the force boundary. Few people were in and the detectives had occupied a table in a shadowy corner of the pub. No one took any notice of them.

'I am afraid so,' nodded Blizzard.

'Some people will believe anything,' commented Alex Mather.

'That's the point,' said Blizzard, taking a sip of his pint. 'St Clair was clever, I'll give him that. He knew that people wanted to believe that something special was happening at St Mary's. It didn't take him long to convince them that it was the Lord's work.'

'In a way,' said Ronald morosely, 'it is worse than many other crimes because he took away their dreams.'

And mine,' grunted Randall, 'because none of it gets us any closer to the sex ring does it?'

'Not really,' admitted Blizzard. 'Although I reckon Macklin was hinting that we were right in his letter. That's how I read that bit about taking his secrets to the grave.'

'Then perhaps,' suggested Mather mischievously, 'it is one for Dennis Barry to investigate, after all.'

'He'd like that, would old Dennis,' smiled Ronald. 'He'll be bored with all those Heavenly choirs by now.'

'Who said he's in Heaven?' asked Blizzard impishly.

'Good point,' said Randall, then turning eyes on Ronald, he asked, 'So, guv, does Keeper continue?'

'Yes,' nodded the superintendent firmly. 'We've learnt enough in the past two weeks to believe more than ever that we are on the right track. We'll get the break one day, I am sure of that.'

'What about that Councillor Gallagher?' asked Mather. 'Do you think he might be in on it?'

'Too in love with himself to bother about anyone else,' grunted Blizzard, and he smiled. 'I'll tell you one thing, though. He was pretty hacked off when I told him that the bishop had taken over the running of St Mary's and decided to close the hostel.'

'I would have paid good money to see the look on his face,' chuckled Ronald.

'I did,' quipped Colley.

When the laughter had subsided, Randall said seriously, 'I reckon you're right, guv—we have to keep Keeper going. Dennis Barry believed there was something to it and that's good enough for me.'

'I'll go with that,' nodded Blizzard and he lifted his pint glass. 'A toast—to absent friends.'

'To absent friends,' they chorused and downed their drinks.

'And,' said Ronald, winking at the others, 'since I am about to sign his overtime claim, I reckon it is time for John to get them in.'

'Some people,' grumbled Blizzard as he gathered up the empty glasses and started off for the bar, 'have no respect.'

We hope you have enjoyed this Large Print book. Other Chivers Press or Thorndike Press Large Print books are available at your library or directly from the publishers.

For more information about current and forthcoming titles, please call or write, without obligation, to:

Chivers Large Print
published by BBC Audiobooks Ltd
St James House, The Square
Lower Bristol Road
Bath BA2 3BH
UK
email: bbcaudiobooks@bbc.co.uk
www.bbcaudiobooks.co.uk

OR

Thorndike Press
295 Kennedy Memorial Drive
Waterville
Maine 04901
USA
www.gale.com/thorndike
www.gale.com/wheeler

All our Large Print titles are designed for easy reading, and all our books are made to last.